After Lydia

After Lydia

SANDRA TYLER

HARCOURT BRACE & COMPANY

NEW YORK   SAN DIEGO   LONDON

Tyler

Requests for permission to make copies of any
part of the work should be mailed to:
Permissions Department, Harcourt Brace & Company,
6277 Sea Harbor Drive, Orlando, Florida 32887-6777

Library of Congress Cataloging-in-Publication Data
Tyler, Sandra.
After Lydia/Sandra Tyler.
p.   cm.
ISBN 0-15-193111-9
I. Title.
PS3570.Y527A68   1995
813'.54—dc20   94-27359

Designed by Lydia D'moch
Printed in the United States of America
A B C D E

In memory of you, Daddy

May you still bring up close for me
the texture of the moment

My deepest gratitude, always, to Cork Smith for his
unwavering faith and perseverance; to Bansie Vasvani
for her great generosity; and to Mary Evans for
continuing to be my guardian angel

After Lydia

CHAPTER 1

IT WAS A LITTLE over a year since Vickie's mother was killed crossing the railroad tracks, carrying only her car keys on a metal, heart-shaped ring. Vickie used to play by the old depot there, now a concession stand. She'd sail oak leaves in the pools of water along the edge of the tracks and draw sweeping shapes in the bright green scum collecting on the surface from the overhanging willows. The keys, along with her wedding ring and the ordinary gold posts her mother had worn, never having cared much for earrings, were returned to the family in a plastic bag.

Vickie hadn't been home in almost five months, not since Christmas, when dried pine needles blanketed their living-room floor because her mother had been the one to water the tree every year. It had rained during the entire drive up from New York, and her head ached from straining to see through the windshield, although usually Vickie liked driving late, after rush hour when she could drive eighty along the endless stretch of glistening asphalt. When the earth seemed flat and she could forget the most she could do was circle around and around the globe.

"So what do you think of your grandmother's T-bird?" her father, Blake, asked, sitting next to her on the couch where he'd been catching up on newspapers while waiting for her to arrive.

"I believe it," Vickie said, peeling off her socks soaked through since she'd stopped for coffee. "She bought that pasta maker and that other thing, some facial steam massage. As if she believed in facials."

"She hasn't driven in over ten years. Not since she tore the muffler off on that rock at the end of the driveway."

"Must you talk about me like I'm not in the room?" Vickie's grandmother Ruth asked, standing beside the blue velvet chair as if waiting for the appropriate moment to excuse herself for bed.

Blake lit a cigarette from the pack he kept on the

end table beside Ruth's collection of mussel shells. "She's even hidden the keys."

"I've always wanted a T-bird," Ruth said, folding her arms on the chair's back as Vickie had seen her lean on lecterns to rally support for finding the tombstones stolen from the graveyard or for stopping the illegal dumping behind the nursing home. She hadn't worked for any cause since Vickie's mother died. She'd gazed at her daughter's things in the plastic bag as if they were something alive and swimming around.

"How can I take it out for a spin if you've hidden the keys?" Vickie asked.

"A 'spin'?" her father said. "Vickie, you don't take cars for a spin. You take them for a drag race."

"You exaggerate."

"You burn rubber."

"No one's taking that car *anywhere,*" Ruth said, scooping up her thirteen-year-old cat. "Guess whose cat door Piper's been using?" Cradling Piper, she came around and settled into the velvet chair with the utmost purpose. "Our new neighbors'. That's how I first met Mrs. Arnold, in fact, when she came by to complain about Piper using their litter box." Ruth grinned, quickly covering her mouth to hide her crooked teeth. "Isn't that marvelous?"

The Arnolds had moved in seven months ago, and Vickie could imagine Ruth scrutinizing them as she would anyone new to Lawton, what had been a small coastal Massachusetts village back when Ruth's great-great-grandmother had been among its earliest settlers.

"She thinks they're Mafia," Blake said, taking a mussel shell and examining it with a scientific thoughtfulness, nudging it in his palm as if he were adjusting it beneath a microscope. If not a scientist, he would be mistaken for a professor rather than the owner of a lamp sales and repair shop.

"They're always doing something to that house," Ruth said. "Who else would ruin that charming back porch by putting in sliding glass doors?"

"But *Mafia,* Gramma?" Vickie said.

"Over in Sladebrook, there was a family just like the Arnolds, with a big house and pool . . . and a month ago they moved out in the middle of the night. A week later, it turned out they were connected with a murder in Florida."

"The Mafia wouldn't have cats," Blake said, turning over the shell so he could drop his cigarette ashes into it. "They'd have guard dogs. Dobermans."

Ruth sank into the chair as if down a shallow hole. "And what do *you* know about the Mafia?"

"About as much as you," he said, laughing.

"How would you know what kind of animals they'd keep? You've been watching too many trashy movies on that hideous machine."

"It's called a VCR. And you've been reading too many trashy tabloids about people moving out in the middle of the night."

Ruth eyed the mussel shell. She had collected the shells from the beach because of their silvery blue interiors, and Vickie knew how she hated Blake using them as ashtrays. "None of it nearly as trashy as *you* are," she said, pushing Piper off her lap to snatch away the shell. "You don't even have the decency not to use my good brandy glasses for a stinking glass of water." She emptied the shell into the fireplace and wiped it out with a tissue from her sleeve. "Always making such a mess all over this house, *my* house."

There wasn't much Blake could say to that. After they were married he and Vickie's mother had moved onto the third floor, where there was a small kitchen, planning to stay there only until they had saved enough for their own place. They were never able to save, and gradually their lives spilled down into the rest of the house. Although Ruth would forever consider the house her own personal domain, Vickie knew she was quite fond of Blake, having long since accepted him as as much of a fixture as her old embroidered sofa. They just argued as much as they always had, their only real way of communicating.

Replacing the shell, Ruth took a moment to rearrange the others, and a silence was draped across them as thick and scratchy as the old woolen army blankets Ruth kept on all their beds to conserve heat on winter nights. It was the same silence that had weighed so heavily on them after the memorial service, when the only thing left to do was vacuum the living room where they'd held the reception. Ruth had knelt to pick out the crumbs from the carpet herself.

"Well . . . ," Ruth said, moving around the room picking things up and putting them down, the assortment of Christmas balls still clustered on the mantel even though it was now the end of May.

Blake began noisily gathering his newspapers. "So your drive was okay? Was quite a storm."

"It took a little longer than usual," Vickie said, her head pounding steadily now.

"I don't know about you all . . . ," he said, his papers crumpled under one arm.

"It *is* late," Ruth said, heading into the kitchen, Vickie knew, for her usual cup of chamomile tea to help ease her insomnia.

Despite her headache, Vickie wished she were back out in the rain speeding through the path of her own headlights.

CHAPTER 2

VICKIE WOKE near dawn and heard Ruth moving through the house looking for something. Her grandmother had always been up nights looking for things: a misplaced watch or glove, an unfinished shopping list. And she'd look in all the wrong places: the watch would be out on the lawn, the glove absently tucked into a bookcase, and the list used as a coaster, found crumpled and stained with an herbal-tea ring on some corner table.

Vickie recognized the sounds of dining-room chairs being moved and the shifting of the silver candlesticks on the sideboard, sounds she'd found comforting growing up in that house. Now they made her uneasy and she stared around her old room, at her walls that in the gray predawn light seemed translucent. She thought she could see the shadow of handprints beneath the paint and remembered her mother showing her how to roll her hands in the various paint trays so that her prints would be rainbow colored. Vickie had thought her mother's own prints were lacy like the cutout snowflakes decorating her classroom windows.

It had been easy to be close to her mother then, close enough to smell the way her clothes still smelled after she died, faintly of chimney smoke and damp wood, a scent all her own. Vickie pulled herself down beneath the blankets longing for her as she used to at night when the prints would seem to inch stealthily across the walls and she'd cry out for her mother.

Back in New York Vickie sometimes imagined she saw her, at Woolworth's trying to decide between flowering cactuses on sale, and once standing on line at the bank taking in and out those gold posts as she would whenever she had to wait. At the Laundromat, a middle-aged woman wearing loafers and a cotton dress had sat leaning her elbows on her knees—Vickie's mother used to wear loafers with cotton dresses and sit like that bent over one of her mystery novels.

But this woman wasn't reading, she was dozing, and Vickie could have been seeing her mother as she really felt. When she wasn't trying to keep her patience with Vickie by running her fingers across the radiators, the only time she ever checked for dust. When what she was feeling was only terribly tired. Tired enough to nod off, to let one arm slip from her lap and dangle uselessly, and Vickie had wanted to go to her—to go to her mother as she never had wanted to when her mother was alive, when they weren't able to stay in the same room long enough for this, to see how each other really felt.

Ruth had moved into the living room; Vickie knew the knock of the brass handles on the highboy as she opened and closed the drawers. Her mother used to get up when she heard Ruth, and then the only sounds would be the slap of cards as they played a game of double solitaire.

Vickie found her grandmother turning over the pillows on the living-room couch.

"A ruby fell out of my pin. I noticed it when I was taking it off tonight," Ruth said.

"That won't be too easy to find."

"No, I suppose I should give up," Ruth said, lifting the magazines on the piano bench.

Vickie didn't remember the piano ever being played, as she didn't remember the grandfather clock in the hall telling the right time, nor the elaborately engraved old toasters lining a shelf in the kitchen ever having actually worked. It was a house full of relics, built by Ruth's great-great-grandfather who was also the original owner of the Lawton clock factory. The house, as well as the factory, had been passed down through the generations, until Ruth sold the factory a year following her husband's death.

She'd made a sizable profit on the sale of the factory, more than enough to afford some improvements on the house, but as far as Vickie knew, she hadn't made a single change except for repapering the living room eleven years ago. And not since Ruth's mother first hung Ruth's grandparents' baby cups in the buffet above an arrangement of family daguerreotypes and displayed Ruth's great-grand-father's snuffboxes in a glass case in Ruth's bedroom had anything been rearranged.

So much of what was in that house was from Ruth's own past that even before Lydia died, there was little to remind Vickie of her mother. In the attic was Lydia's old rocking horse and a couple of china dolls, but anything of real value that belonged to Lydia as an adult seemed to have been inherited— the jewelry she'd left to Vickie and her sister was their great-great-grandmother's engagement ring, her charm bracelet of old coins, and an elephant-hair necklace.

Ruth sat heavily on the couch, seeming resigned. Everything about her was tiny; her eyes were the startled beady eyes of a squirrel, and her hands twitched slightly, kneading one of the pillows like the nimble paws of a raccoon. "How could anything wake you after that long drive in that torrential rain? And your father sitting by the window rustling the paper like he does . . . He hates so your driving in the dark."

"I can't help it, it's quicker after rush hour."

"He's right about that little Honda—it could be whipped right off the road."

"Well, it's got to be safer than that beat-up old T-bird."

Ruth combed the pillow's fringe. "You know, I don't want this party."

"You love parties," Vickie said, suddenly afraid. As afraid as when in New York she'd find herself staring at nothing but old ironing boards, typewriters, and warped tables in the Salvation Army window on Eighth Avenue.

"I don't understand it, where it could have fallen out," Ruth said, getting up to search through the cluster of Christmas balls.

It was hard to imagine Ruth not wanting a party. If there was music, she'd be the first to dance. Most of all, she liked to gather a crowd around her so that she could launch into some dull story only she could make interesting, about hallucinating while having her neck bent too far back over the sink at the beauty parlor and seeing large, bulbous fish eyes.

Vickie had wondered, though, whether Ruth would really feel like celebrating, despite the fact that it had been a full year now since the accident. It had been Vickie's sister's idea to throw her an eightieth birthday party.

"Mom, I think, would want you to have it, Gramma," Vickie said.

Ruth's face lost all expression, and Vickie was reminded of how she'd spent that first month after the funeral in bed knitting, something for which she'd never had patience. She didn't knit anything in particular, crooked squares she'd unravel again and again until the yarn was worn thin as thread. She got out of bed only when she discovered one of her tortoiseshell combs was missing, and she wandered around the house, mumbling, "I told her, I warned her, I always warned her, that bend, oh, that bend . . ."

The "bend" was where the tracks veered sharply to the west and seemed to disappear, the reason why Vickie's mother had forbidden her to play there. But Lydia was not the only one to avoid the town's traffic by parking in the old station lot and to stop at the concession stand for its famous raspberry ice cream before crossing the tracks to Main Street. That day, she'd run out of fertilizer while planting new hydrangea bushes and, rarely bothering with her purse when she had only one errand, she'd grabbed a few loose dollars along with the car keys. She'd told Ruth she'd be right back.

When Vickie used to sail leaves in those green pools of water, at least she could hear the whistle if she couldn't actually see the train. Even when the wind was blowing from the east, and she didn't think she could hear it at all. Again and again, when she'd find herself longing so for her mother, when she'd be grappling with the fact that she could be so abruptly, simply gone, it would seem impossible that her mother hadn't known the train was coming.

Vickie sat on the embroidered couch, the pattern of roses long since shredded by a succession of cats over the years. "Gramma, do you still think about it?"

"Think about what, Victoria?" Ruth was the only one in the family who called everyone by their full names, and if piqued, she'd place special emphasis on specific syllables.

Vickie was unable to look at her, as if she'd been caught handling those snuffboxes Ruth never allowed her to touch. "About what happened."

"Of course I think about it."

"Well, wouldn't she have heard it? When I played down there—"

"You *played* down there? Your mother never

allowed you down there. . . . I wouldn't allow *her,* and she knew enough not to."

For as far back as Vickie could remember, her grandmother had been reminding her of what a good, thoughtful daughter Lydia had always been, from the time Lydia's father died when she was only nine, and every morning she brushed and braided Ruth's hair. Lydia not only would never have deceived her mother by playing on the tracks, but she wouldn't have hid cigarettes in her room or cut school and certainly never lied about going to theater rehearsals when she was secretly meeting a boyfriend twice her age.

"Maybe she played down there, anyway," Vickie said. "I mean, she wouldn't tell you, would she?"

Vickie waited for Ruth's cheeks to become spotted with red as they invariably would when she was made angry. Instead, she looked as bewildered as when she'd pressed her hands against the display cabinet at the funeral parlor, trying to choose between the various ornate urns, and Vickie felt guilty for having brought up the accident at all.

Ruth looked out the window, saying, "You haven't seen what else the Arnolds have done to that house."

"Besides the sliding doors?" Vickie asked, relieved to have the subject changed.

"That was only the last time you were home, how many months ago?"

Vickie didn't say anything. She hadn't come home for Easter, worried she might come to blows with her sister as she almost had at Christmas. Meryl had tried so hard to disguise their mother's absence. She'd draped Ruth's house in tinsel, something Vickie knew she'd always thought tacky, and even had them all sing Christmas carols, trying to bang out a few notes on the old, nearly soundless piano.

"You'll see in the morning—all that charming red shingling? They've put up this horrible brick."

Vickie laughed. "Who ever heard of a godfather named Arnold?"

Ruth came away from the window and sank into the velvet chair. "You didn't have to come home."

"I wouldn't miss your party."

Ruth smirked, kneading the arm.

"I wanted to come home."

"Don't be silly, dear."

Somewhere there was a gurgling in a pipe, what Ruth called one of the house's laments.

"Did you look in the rug?" Vickie asked, kneeling to rake her fingertips through the fibers.

CHAPTER 3

VICKIE RARELY looked forward to coming home except to catch up with her old boyfriend, Kyle. Until she met him, growing up in Lawton had been like being trapped in a dressing room walled with mirrors. She'd had to go to the private school that her mother, grandmother, and great-grandmother had attended before her, and everywhere she turned, she'd catch some new disfavorable angle of herself, a side that further proved her unable to fit into the expected garb.

She'd been running away from that town since

she was thirteen and had cut school to spend a day in Boston. At eighteen she took off backpacking through Arizona and New Mexico. No one in her family had been able to understand the allure of the deep red earth of Canyon de Chelly and the shimmering white sands of the Enchanted Mesa. Her mother, especially, couldn't understand why Vickie felt so compelled to go off by herself in the first place. "Why not the mountains?" she'd said. "At least there's some shade in the mountains."

Vickie could hear what her mother would have to say now if she knew Vickie had quit her job at Wendel's, a small publishing house in New York where she'd recently been promoted to an assistant designer. When Vickie had announced she was dropping out of college to pursue a career in photography, Lydia had said, "Why do you insist on squandering your gifts? Your God-given gifts?" She'd assumed Vickie would become a premed at New York University where she had been a biology major, since Vickie had done especially well in the sciences all through high school. Ruth, the one to cover her tuition, argued that Vickie was "spoiled."

And after that, Vickie refused even loans from her grandmother, managing to support herself doing shoots for various gourmet and travel magazines. When she gave up photography, she assisted a dog trainer for a couple of years until she figured out what she really wanted to do. Later, she took graphic design classes and managed to put together an impressive enough portfolio to land her an entry-level job at Wendel's.

After four years at Wendel's, Vickie was finally doing some actual designing of book jackets, but of course now she'd given that up too, and she wasn't exactly sure why—something she never would have admitted to her mother. She had less reasoned the decision than made it instinctively, as she made most decisions such as packing away the knickknacks in her apartment so that all surfaces reminded her of freshly cleared ice-skating rinks.

From the living-room window, Vickie looked out at Ruth who sat in her Thunderbird sipping her morning's coffee. She was drinking from one of her best cups, the hand-painted ones decorated with yellow butterflies, cups she never allowed anyone to use, even herself. The car was parked so that it faced the Arnolds', and Ruth had to keep her chin lifted to see above the dashboard.

"If she was going to go and buy an old car like that, she should have gotten a Hawk," Blake said, drinking his own coffee from a chipped mug and sitting in the rocking chair Ruth didn't like him to sit in because of the sagging seat. "The Studebaker Hawk, *there* was a car. But, no, she had to have a convertible. She had to have those silver fins."

Earlier that morning, his door had been open

enough for Vickie to see him sitting on the edge of his bed. He was facing away from her and by the way his head was bowed, she thought he was crying. Then she'd heard the faint click of scissors and knew he was only clipping his fingernails.

"What was she thinking, anyway?" Vickie asked.

"All I know is, she saw an ad posted somewhere and had to have that car. So she can sit in it like it's some kind of *lounge* chair."

It was a particularly warm day, but Ruth wore her daughter's salmon lamb's wool sweater—being so thin, she was always cold. It was one of the few things they'd kept of Lydia's, and Vickie was a little surprised that her grandmother would actually wear it. But when they'd finally gone through Lydia's clothes, Ruth had been the one to systematically empty her drawers. "You know she never cared about anything nice, anyway, those good dresses she'd wear all rumpled to the club," Ruth had reminded Vickie, who watched numbly from the doorway.

"Gramma said she didn't want this party," Vickie said, sitting on the couch.

"I don't think she knows what she wants these days, except that old car," Blake said, lighting a cigarette. "And your sister's gone to an awful lot of trouble, too, what with even renting that hall."

The hall was a large converted barn with a capacity to hold two hundred people.

"You know Meryl—look at the parties she gives every year for the kids." Last year, she'd sent Vickie pictures of the pony she'd rented for rides around her backyard.

"Those kids. All the time she spends planning things and making us chicken soup, she should be keeping track of her children."

"Chicken soup?"

"Alex is always off on her bike somewhere, especially now that school's out."

"So was I at eleven."

"Ten. She's only ten."

"I'd bike over to that abandoned duck farm, or hide out in that old boathouse on Bell Lake," Vickie said.

"See? We never knew where *you* were, either."

Ruth had one arm stretched along the door and the other gripping the wheel as if she were imagining herself cruising down some coastal freeway.

"What's this about chicken soup?" Vickie asked.

"Meryl's been making us huge vats of it as if we both have the flu. I'm surprised they have any chickens left at all, with all that soup. Speaking of, did she tell you about the massacre? A dog came through and killed six of them. Glenn said next time he's going to shoot it."

"He wouldn't shoot a dog."

20

"It's legal. He gets fifteen dollars from the dog warden for every head."

"It's not like it's his business," Vickie said. "If Ruth hadn't cut out that article about unsanitary poultry inspections . . ."

Blake shrugged. "Fifteen dollars is fifteen dollars." He was sitting next to the old piano and, reaching over, he drummed on one of the yellowed keys. It made no more than a faint tinkling sound. "So how's the city?"

"The city? The city's fine."

"How can the city be fine, what with all those water main breaks and that subway crash—that island's tipping, if you ask me, and one day it's going to sink to the bottom of the ocean."

"I thought you were asking about my life. How my life was."

"I am." He shifted so that Vickie could hear the chair's seat straining. "Everything's all right then?"

"I'm leaving Wendel's."

Blake took a shell for his ashes. "You've gotten a better offer?"

"No . . . I'm just leaving. I've already got some freelance work lined up though." She didn't tell him the work was only for a couple of newsletters, enough income to cover one month's rent.

When her father didn't say anything, she turned away from the window. He was shaking his head amusedly.

"What's funny?"

"I've heard this before, that's all."

She wasn't prepared for such nonresistance coming from her father. Although Blake was the most understanding of her family, he hadn't always been exactly supportive. He could obsess about her financial security as he had obsessed about her becoming trapped in a fire that one year in college, because she didn't have a rope ladder to hang out her dorm window.

"You're not going to make me write up a list of pros and cons?"

"Oh, I'm not worried about you, Vickie. You've always turned out okay. Anyway, who am *I* to tell you how to lead your life?"

It was the first time she remembered her father sounding the least bit regretful, so she asked, "What do you wish, you'd done only what it was your father wanted?"

"Well . . . and your mother."

Before opening the lamp store, Blake had been a partner in his father's law firm. After his father died, Blake held together the firm for another year until one week he didn't go into the office at all. He took to the divan in Ruth's great-grandmother's old room on the third floor with what he claimed was a stomach virus. Vickie was seven then, and after school she'd sit on the floor by the divan and together they made an entire flock of paper birds.

One afternoon he wasn't on the divan. He was dressed and standing in her room while her mother was making Vickie's bed—it was the spring day she'd decided to exchange their flannel sheets for cotton ones.

Sharply shaking out a sheet, Lydia said, "Daddy's decided to dissolve the firm."

"Dissolve?" Vickie asked. Dissolve meant powdered Kool-Aid stirred into a pitcher of water.

"He doesn't want to be a lawyer anymore."

Blake watched the sheet billow then fall across the mattress as if Lydia were performing some magic trick.

"What do you want to be, Daddy?"

"He doesn't know," Lydia said. "He hasn't a *clue.*"

Vickie realized then that her father hadn't actually been sick lying on the divan. But it wasn't until later, when she'd visit him at his shop and see him bent over his worktable, rewiring some lamp with that scientific thoughtfulness, that she fully understood he'd never wanted to be a lawyer in the first place.

Blake tentatively touched his scalp. His hair had begun to thin and he'd developed a habit of checking the receding lines. "I wish you'd talk to Meryl."

"About Alex?"

"About the soup. It's utterly tasteless. There's

no room for anything else in the refrigerator, and we have to dump it out in the woods."

"I can't tell her that."

"Just tell her not to worry about us. She worries over us so now."

"Does she need to?"

He plucked a loose thread from his cuff. "We can take care of ourselves, Vickie."

She wished she could talk to him about her mother as she had tried to talk to Ruth, but she couldn't bring herself to as she watched him wind the thread around and around his index finger before breaking it off, reminded of how, since Lydia's death, he could spend a good half hour refilling the salt and pepper shakers.

Vickie looked back out the window at her grandmother. Ruth waved wildly as if she'd just arrived back from her long coastal drive. With her elbows crooked like untucked wings, she zigzagged madly up to the house, moving as aimlessly as the sandpipers dodging the tide at Lawton Beach.

"Isn't she a dream?" Ruth asked, coming into the living room.

"Not like the Hawk," Blake said, getting up to empty the mussel shell into the fireplace. "Or the Avanti—now *there* was a car, all fiberglass and with wire wheels."

"What are you thinking all that time out there, Gramma?" Vickie asked.

"She wasn't thinking, she was watching the Arnolds," Blake said.

Ruth frowned, rubbing her bifocals on her sleeve only to rehook them into her collar. "It's a perfect day to spring-clean."

"Since when do you spring-clean?" Vickie laughed.

"Your uncle's flying in tomorrow," Blake said. "You know how he'll do his usual inspection."

Every time he came, Uncle Warren would remind them of how the house had become more and more dilapidated. He was an architect and had been wanting to remodel the old place for years.

"We never would have known the antenna was down at Christmas, if it wasn't for my son," Ruth said.

"And he only calls when there's a hurricane to make sure we have fresh batteries in our flashlights," Blake said, lighting another cigarette. "Even now."

Ruth fingered the bifocals as if she was about to take them out again, but then Alex was standing in the archway.

Vickie hadn't heard the door and she wondered how long her niece had been there, twirling a strand of plastic pearls and clutching a pink box.

"Alexandra, come sit! Come sit!" Ruth exclaimed, settling into the velvet chair and slapping her lap. "Oh, but you better first go give your aunt Victoria a big kiss. Goodness knows, you haven't seen *her* in a while."

"Alex, you shouldn't keep appearing like this," Blake said. "That's almost two miles."

"Want to see my bones?" Alex asked, opening the pink box on Vickie's lap.

It was a makeup box and inside were folding trays and a pop-up mirror. Small skulls of sparrows and fish and even a dried seahorse were organized into the compartments.

"I like this best," Vickie said, admiring the sea-horse.

"Of course you do," Alex said, sounding disappointed. "Because it's perfect. None of the others are perfect."

"We think she's going to be a paleontologist," Blake said.

Alex frowned, suddenly seeming older and wiser than the rest of them. "*No,* I'm *not,*" she said, snapping shut the box. "Can I play in the closet?" she asked, already heading into the hall.

Growing up, Vickie too had liked crawling through the closet that opened from the hall onto the den, although the passage could prove quite treacherous, through beach chairs, old games, and picnic coolers.

"That closet hasn't been cleaned out since I don't know when," Ruth said.

"You say that every year," Blake said.

"Well, then, we'll clean it out today."

"Of course," Blake said. "That's the first place your son will look."

"You're hardly fair."

"You know how long he's been wanting to revamp that closet with fancy drawers and automatic lighting."

"That's how architects *think,* Blake."

In a few minutes, Alex came shuffling into the room in a pair of too-big shoes, ivory pumps with translucent orange stones sewn into the toes.

"Alex!" Ruth exclaimed. "Oh, those shoes, I'd forgotten those shoes," she said, heading into the hall.

Opening one of the many shoe boxes stacked against one side of the closet, she asked, "Where did Lydia ever think she'd wear all these?"

Alex was turning her feet this way and that in front of the coatrack mirror, and Vickie remembered her mother parading up and down the hall. The sight of her in the gaudy pumps would send Vickie and Meryl into a fit of giggles, it having been more like their mother to wear those practical brown loafers. Lydia would laugh, too, as if she'd bought the shoes only for that, to entertain her daughters on a dull afternoon. Ruth would accuse her of being extravagant, but Lydia would shrug, saying, "They caught my eye." She'd take them off for her daughters to try on, and Vickie and her sister would admire themselves in the hall mirror. At the sight of her granddaughters in the too-big shoes, Ruth would have to leave before her face broke out into one of her grins.

Piper got into the closet, toppling the board games. "Oh, you big old cat," Ruth said, sounding more relieved than annoyed. "I can't keep you out of anything. Look at all this junk in here," she said, tossing out badminton rackets.

"We used to have those big games on the Fourth, remember?" Blake said, as if he'd actually played badminton himself. He preferred to watch, stretched out on the lawn with a martini.

"We certainly could use the extra room in here," Ruth said, now tossing out the shoe boxes, and Vickie was reminded of her emptying Lydia's drawers.

"You going to give them all away?" Vickie asked.

"She never *wore* them, Victoria."

"*I'll* wear them."

Alex giggled as Vickie slipped on a lemon-yellow pair, dotted with silver beads.

Blake was leaning on the chest as if for support. He'd only been amused by the shoes and would dare

Lydia to wear them to the club. "I should get going, over to the shop." He wandered upstairs.

Vickie looked at herself in the coatrack mirror and saw Ruth behind her. She'd picked out a pair of pumps herself as if she might actually try them on.

She merely slipped them onto her hands, holding them together in a steeple, and Vickie remembered something. She remembered Ruth adjusting the hem of Lydia's dress for a club Christmas dinner while Lydia stood on a chair. Lydia had stood entirely still, not even taking in and out her gold posts, and Vickie had clearly been able to imagine her as a young girl, as truly being the good daughter Ruth had always claimed her to have been.

Vickie took off the shoes, disappointed that the pumps didn't suit her any more than they had suited her mother.

"All these shoes," Ruth said, shaking her head. "It doesn't make any sense."

"Neither does getting hit by a train," Vickie said.

Ruth's face became as expressionless as earlier in that gray predawn light, and Vickie said, "Oh, I'm sorry, Gramma."

Ruth let the shoes slip off her hands. "You can drive your niece home. I'm sure Meryl would like to know where her daughter is."

CHAPTER 4

VICKIE DIDN'T KNOW why she was thinking so much about the accident— whether it had been an accident at all. She thought her mother would at least have left a note, some kind of explanation, since Lydia could be silly and extravagant—as she was in buying all those shoes—but also extremely practical. When the furnace had spewed thick black smoke, and Ruth could only yell "My house! My house!" weaving in circles out on the lawn, it was Lydia who called the fire department and even thought to shut the basement door so that soot wouldn't blacken the furniture.

It was hard to imagine her mother going to such extremes anyway, rarely having doubted herself except around Ruth who, however subtly, had her say in how Lydia should be raising her children. "All they do is color in pictures of Jesus. It wouldn't hurt them to sit through a sermon," Ruth said whenever Lydia wanted Vickie and Meryl to join the other children for Sunday school. Lydia gave in to Ruth anyway, although not without sneaking them each a Matchbox car to roll quietly along the cushioned pew.

For the most part, there was a sureness about her. She became licensed as a real estate agent to supplement Blake's income after he quit the firm, and she liked to boast about being the one in her office who drew the best bids on the hardest sales. "You know that McFee place we've been trying to get rid of for over a year?" she'd said, coming home one evening and unbuttoning her blouse there in the hall, anxious to get out of one of the stiff linen suits she so hated.

"This house doesn't even have a laundry room, but I could tell this couple wanted sun, so I played up the big bay windows." Taking off her scarf and brandishing it as she started upstairs, she said, "I guess I just know how to size people up."

If there was anything that made Lydia particularly unhappy, it was probably her marriage—Vickie didn't think her mother had ever forgiven Blake for abandoning his practice. After he quit the firm, he took a job selling tags for a label company until he decided that he wanted to open a lamp shop, and they sank the money they had been saving for their own house into setting up the store.

Although Lydia did have a knack for selling houses, the sales were few and far between and her percentage of the commission meager. Waving a fan of private school and orthodontist bills that Ruth herself usually wound up covering, she would remind Blake that her father hadn't liked his own job managing the Lawton clock factory, but nor did he ever forget that he had a family to support. He never would have tolerated having his own mother-in-law paying his family's bills. "And he was lucky enough to have a lucrative clock factory dropped into his lap," Blake would reply. Not having much she could say to that, Lydia would end up dumping the bills into the basket on Ruth's desk.

Over the years though, it was an argument that became as built into their relationship as their habits of sipping an after-dinner cognac from the same glass and flossing their teeth together during the eleven o'clock news. Habits that Vickie knew were ingrained in something deeper than merely routine; sometimes she'd hear both their voices coming from the bathroom in the middle of the night, and in the morning she'd find traces of wax from her mother's favorite vanilla-scented candles along the tub's rim.

Maybe she was thinking so much about the accident only because she'd never really been able to know her mother. She'd never wanted to know her, from the time her mother began searching her room, something Vickie figured out by how her tarot cards and rock crystals were the least bit rearranged. Vickie didn't yet actually have anything to hide, like her cigarettes and birth control pills later on, but her mother worried that there must be something else going on with Vickie besides her being more interested in fortune telling and healing powers than attending sleep-over parties.

The last time Vickie ever saw her mother was two weeks before she died, when the daffodils were finally showing their heads through the old, gray snow along Ruth's front walk. It was the morning after Easter, and Vickie was loading her car to drive back to New York. Lydia stood at the edge of the lawn in her gardening sweater, an old brown thing that was pilling badly and made her look twice her age. She clutched it against her as she stooped to pick up a tiny purple man attached to a plastic parachute.

"Must be Alex's, from one of our shopping sprees," she said, shaking out the crumpled, torn parachute. Lydia was a younger version of Ruth, everything about her as tiny, but with the habit of waving her arms in sweeping gestures that lent her a larger presence. She flung the parachute into the air and laughed as it was turned inside out like a broken umbrella.

She seemed at her most generous when she was able to forget herself like that, and Vickie tried to make the parachute work herself. The little purple man spiraled crazily before plunging to the ground, and they were both laughing now.

Remembering herself, Lydia carefully wrapped the parachute around the man and tucked the neat bundle into her pocket. "I hope you're careful."

Vickie felt the old resentment returning. Although Vickie was at least three inches taller and bigger-boned, Lydia could seem to tower above her. "No U-turns, only seat belts," Vickie said.

"You know what I mean."

Her whole body tensed as it would when her mother began like this. All weekend, they'd been arguing on and off about Vickie protesting against pro-life demonstrators forming human barriers outside abortion clinics. Whether Vickie was helping with the dishes or hiding chocolate eggs for Alex, her mother would bring up the subject again and again. "Only God can determine when a life is truly viable," Lydia had said, tucking an egg behind the grandfather clock.

Vickie knew it wasn't so much the actual issue that was upsetting to her mother, as the fact that

Vickie was proving herself as much a source of worry as she'd always been.

"What do you really think's going to happen to me?" Vickie asked.

"You can get so carried away, Vickie."

"It's called having convictions."

Her mother laughed, but not in the way she had laughed tossing the parachute. "And you have so *many* convictions," she said, waving her hands around in a sweeping arc.

"And I also have a crooked middle finger and astigmatism in my left eye."

Lydia looked startled, and Vickie was as pleased as when at fourteen she first really shocked her by lighting up a cigarette at the breakfast table; before ceremoniously flushing the cigarette down the toilet, her mother had looked at her in the same way.

The startled look faded more quickly than it used to, and Lydia fingered the torn threads where the buttons were gone on her sweater, as she would when someone unexpectedly appeared at the front door and caught her looking like that.

"I'll be careful, Mom," Vickie said, kissing her.

Lydia made no move to touch her.

Vickie got in the car, anxious to be on the road. Her final image of her mother was in the rearview mirror—she'd taken out the bundle and was turning it over in her hands.

Vickie squeezed Alex's bike into the back of her Honda to drive her niece home. The town had changed a lot over the years, having doubled in size due to the growing number of summer people. Ruth had petitioned against the movie theater and Wal-Mart, but Vickie wished they'd been built long ago. Except for a hardware store, the A&P, a couple of restaurants, and a few boutiques open primarily during the summer season, they'd have to drive to Slade-brook for everything else, and groups of kids would climb onto a local bus to hang out at the video arcade at the mall there.

Ruth would tell and retell stories about what Lawton had been like before the fields were sold off for summer developments and when the clock factory was the mainstay of employment. Back in the time of Ruth's great-great-grandmother, there wasn't even a church, and she had to ride a horse and buggy to Sladebrook for Sunday services.

Some things hadn't changed and seemed like anachronisms, especially the country club whose membership had dwindled down to mostly Ruth's generation. The yacht club, having expanded its facilities to include tennis courts and a small golf range, attracted the newest members. The neon sign of a dolphin still hung outside the Dolphin's pizza parlor although it had long since burned out. And the large brass clock face still hung above the main door to

the factory, even though the factory closed down
only ten years after Ruth sold it. It was now the
public lower school, and Vickie wished she'd been
able to go there, having hated her private school
where Alex now went.

Passing the old brick building, it didn't seem
quite so daunting as Vickie remembered. "Don't
suppose Mrs. Kent's still there—she used to inspect
our fingernails every day."

"I had to bring in a nailbrush," Alex said.

"You're kidding. She must be . . . God, I don't
know how old."

"She's a big old witch."

Every day, Mrs. Kent would inspect their fingernails and Vickie too was told to bring in a brush.
Her mother had been furious, but instead of confronting the teacher, every morning before school
Lydia herself inspected Vickie's nails.

"Does your mom know that? That she told you
to bring in a brush?"

"You drive better than her," Alex said, folding
her hands neatly on top of her makeup box.

"Your mother?"

"Sometimes she'll pass two cars at once."

It was hard for Vickie to imagine her overly cau-
tious sister passing even one car; Meryl would take
forever turning into traffic.

"Look! Can we stop?" Alex yelled, as they passed
the A&P's parking lot where a lake had formed from

last night's rain. "You think there are fish in there?" Alex asked.

"Not unless a trout or two fell from the sky."

"If they left the water, things might start to grow," Alex said, sounding miffed. "Can we go wading?"

"That's probably not such a good idea," Vickie said, knowing Meryl would worry about her daughter stepping on broken glass. But Vickie couldn't resist the idea and pulled into the lot.

The lake was being pumped out by a man wearing a hat covered with smiley buttons, and he watched them suspiciously. Vickie didn't care, becoming as entranced by the ripplings of the water as she could be wading into the bay. "So where do you go when you go off on your bike?"

Alex held her face close to the surface as if still expecting to see fish. "Different places . . ."

"There's an old boathouse on Bell Lake I used to go to."

Stumbling, Alex laughed and caught herself on Vickie's arm.

"I used to climb through this window, and inside I'd pretend it was my own little house."

Alex looked at her a moment, then leaned down to swirl her hands in the water. "You know, I've never been to New York," she said, sounding older and wiser.

"You'll have to visit me."

"Yeah?"

"Yeah," Vickie said, although she knew her sister would never agree to it, at least not without first reciting the latest in subway crime statistics. "I can take you to a ball game. You'll have to promise to root for the Mets, though."

"It's all boarded up now."

"What is?"

"The boathouse. You can't get in." Alex stepped daintily out of the water, bunching up her shorts like the folds of some long, full skirt. "Well, you almost can't, anyway."

CHAPTER 5

MERYL WAS SPREADING newspapers across her kitchen floor to paint the cabinets. She and her husband, Glenn, had been working on their house since they bought it when they first married, and Vickie couldn't imagine their ever actually finishing it. Besides adding on a couple of rooms in the back, Glenn had opened up the living room by tearing down the kitchen wall and putting in a counter with stools.

"I can't believe Gramma still has so many friends left you'd have to rent out a hall," Vickie said.

"Well, they're not *all* her friends," Meryl said, checking a turkey roasting in the oven for the party. "But they're people she sees every day, people she's fond of, like the cashier at Cray's Deli."

"You invited the cashier? From *Cray's?*"

"She goes in there almost every day, Vickie, and talks up a storm. And then there are her old friends from the church, poor Ginger Markson who's got that carpal tunnel syndrome and both arms in casts from too many years of needlepointing."

"You're painting the cabinets when you have the party to get ready for?" Vickie asked.

"Take a peek in the fridge, why don't you."

Besides another turkey, there were two cooked hams, cheeses, and rolls of salami.

"This will all keep?" Vickie asked.

"Of course it will keep, it's only a couple of days." Tossing a pile of toast crusts out the window for the chickens, Meryl said, "What Glenn does down in that barn all morning, I don't know. By the time he gets over to the house it's already after noon."

Glenn was building a spec house, and their barn was filled with antique staircases and old floorboards he'd collected from demolition companies. Piled along their driveway were sinks and lion-footed bathtubs. There were also things he might never use: a dentist's chair and mirrors as big as tabletops leaning up against the house. He had worked for a contractor before he decided to go out on his own.

"Seems like yesterday he was digging out the foundation," Vickie said.

"It was over a *year* ago."

"Aunt Vickie said I can visit her in the city," Alex said. She'd spread out her bones across the couch as if working out some kind of secret pattern.

Meryl looked at her sister with disapproval. "Oh?"

"Can't I?"

"We'll have to see, sweetie," Meryl said distractedly, gathering up measuring cups, plastic soup bowls, and teaspoons from the floor. "Daryll never plays with anything we buy anymore." Her two-year-old was taking a nap.

Except for weight she'd put on around her hips, Meryl seemed as elastic as she'd been when she was on the gymnastics team back in high school. Vickie had deeply envied her limberness then, her compact little body; Vickie's height and big-bonedness came from their father, and people always assumed she was the older sister. Meryl was also graced with Ruth's and their mother's fine freckled features and tiny wrists, that delicacy boys had found so enticing.

But it was a delicacy that betrayed a fierceness that could sting like a slap in the face. When they were growing up, it was Meryl who put an abrupt end to any family bickering, appearing in the room banging pie tins together or hitting the andirons with the poker. At other times, it was a fierceness that only seemed able to translate itself into a cleaning frenzy—Meryl would be the one most inspired to spring-clean. Until the rest of the family took pity and helped, Meryl would try to lift the furniture and drag out the rugs to be aired like an ant trying to manage too large crumbs.

Considering how neat Meryl had always been, her place was as cluttered as Ruth's house, although a lot of the stuff belonged to Glenn; the bookshelves he'd built were lined not with books but with things for the spec house, various old kitchen faucets, porcelain doorknobs, scraps of tile, and frosted glass lampshades.

"Where are you going now?" Meryl asked.

"Just *outside*," Alex said.

Meryl looked out at her daughter through the screen door. She wiped her hands on her oversize shirt patterned with blurry lime-green frogs, something one of the kids must have made. "I don't know where she goes."

"She told me she goes to some of my old haunts," Vickie said.

"She *told* you that?"

"Not exactly . . . she alluded to it," Vickie said, wondering whom she was betraying more, Alex or her sister. "And she also told me Mrs. Kent still makes the kids bring in nailbrushes."

"It happened only once."

"Did you say anything?"

"To who?"

"Mrs. Kent."

"Mrs. Kent's just being Mrs. Kent. She's a good teacher, just . . . meticulous."

"She's humiliating. The only reason she wasn't to you was because you had no nails, bitten down to the quick."

"The point is, it hasn't happened again, Vickie."

"Because now you're the one inspecting her nails like Mom used to?"

"White will make the place look so much bigger, don't you think?" Meryl said, handing Vickie a brush. "We'll start with the ones under the sink."

Vickie wondered at how she still found herself doing what Meryl told her, as if their five-year age difference was as pronounced as when Meryl was beginning to wear bras and she'd snatch away some small pink one Vickie might pick up from her bed.

"Did you tell Dad?" Meryl asked.

Vickie had already told Meryl over the phone about quitting her job, having always consulted with her before she had to confront her parents. Although Meryl certainly had never approved of her decisions any more than had her parents, she was better able to gauge their reactions.

"He was actually good about it."

Meryl laughed. "I guess he's finally grown used to your crazy ways."

"It wasn't what I wanted to be doing, Mel."

"You'd just gotten that promotion. And benefits—what are you doing now about insurance?"

"I've got emergency medical."

"That doesn't cover a thing. What if you have to have surgery?"

"I'm not going to have to have surgery."

"That's what Lisa said, and then one morning she just didn't wake up, had gone into a coma." Lisa was the receptionist at the eye clinic where Meryl worked part-time as an optician's assistant. "It was a bone infection in her skull and she had to have a metal plate put in." Meryl hoarded disaster stories like the rubber bands and plastic-bag twisters Vickie knew she couldn't bear to waste.

"It wasn't what I wanted to be *doing*, Meryl."

If they had been back in school, Vickie would have slammed her bedroom door in Meryl's face by now. Meryl would come in anyway, and Vickie would bury her head beneath her pillow. When Vickie had refused to attend confirmation classes, she barricaded the door with her desk.

"You're acting really stupid," Meryl had said, tapping her nails against the door as if considering clawing her way in.

"To you it's stupid."

"You're just rebelling for the sake of rebelling, Victoria."

Meryl rarely called her by her full name except when she was acting particularly self-righteous. "This isn't worth this," she said, and Vickie knew she meant it wasn't worth upsetting their mother who was downstairs banging open and shut the kitchen drawers.

"I'm just not a hypocrite, like you."

Meryl didn't say anything; she held no more real religious beliefs than Vickie, but when it had been Meryl's time to be confirmed, Vickie couldn't imagine her even having contemplated going against their mother's wishes.

"So what is it you want to do?" Meryl asked.

"I don't know, maybe go back to college."

"You hated college."

"You're right. Maybe I'll go to Australia then."

"Australia? What's in Australia?"

Vickie had no desire to go to Australia, but she enjoyed the note of alarm in her sister's voice. "Aborigines. Caves. I wouldn't mind living in a cave."

Meryl frowned. "Sorry. You just don't seem to stick with any one thing for very long, at least not long enough to really know. Like Ted—I never understood what happened with him."

Ted was someone Vickie had gone out with for a couple of months. "It just burned out."

"That's not the first time you've said that, that it just burned out."

"He alphabetized his soup cans, Mel."

Meryl laughed. "Well, he sounds stable anyway. The kind of guy who won't throw you a curve, like investing your life's savings in a piece of land no one wants to live on."

Vickie was surprised, remembering how supportive Meryl had been when Glenn bought the property. "You always said that was the best investment you ever made."

"It was. I mean, I thought it was . . ." Meryl scratched her cheek, leaving a smudge of white. "The thing is, Glenn didn't stop to consider why that land was so cheap in the first place. It's the first house on the block, that's why, and any prospective buyers we've seen so far don't want to worry about living through the construction of the rest of the block. On top of that, we've had to pay for the installation of all the electrical wiring on the street. And the market's gotten so bad, we'll have to come down in price anyway."

"Well, the market's not Glenn's fault."

Meryl didn't say anything, and Vickie reached to wipe Meryl's cheek but the paint had already dried. "That was as much your idea as it was Glenn's, Mel. You were the one to talk Gramma into that loan—"

"He's always wanted to be his own contractor.

He's always wanted to be his own *boss*." Meryl pointed at Vickie's cabinet with her brush. "You missed some spots."

"I'm taking a break," Vickie said, dropping her brush, tired of Meryl always changing the subject when Vickie might actually be proving her wrong.

She sat on the couch. The coffee table was something Glenn had made, a piece of glass fitted over a slab of marble, and beneath the glass was a collage of photographs. "Dad feels you've been fussing too much over them."

"He said that?"

"Why are you making them all this chicken soup?"

"They haven't been eating right," Meryl said, making a production out of peeling Vickie's brush away from the newspaper. "Gramma's so thin."

"Gramma's always been thin."

"And Dad's eating all the wrong things like frozen veal patties for lunch."

"They're doing all right, Mel."

"And how would *you* know, Victoria?"

Cringing at that self-righteous tone, Vickie looked out at Alex. She'd climbed onto the electrical wire spool Glenn had brought home for her to use as a play table.

Vickie knew Meryl didn't understand any more than did Ruth why she couldn't have come home for both Easter and the party. At Christmas, Meryl had reprimanded Vickie for "sulking" when she refused to join in the singing of carols.

"They're both just rattling around that house," Meryl said. "Gramma is so preoccupied with that car, and when Dad's not at the shop, he's puttering around in the basement."

"He's always been puttering around in the basement."

Meryl dabbed at the spots Vickie had missed.

"Maybe he should start meeting people," Vickie said.

"You mean date?"

"He's not meant to be alone," Vickie said.

Meryl nodded.

"I tried talking to Gramma about Mom. She can't talk about it at all."

"It's been a year, Vickie."

"I know it's been a year."

"So you have to let it go."

"Have *you* let it go?"

Meryl didn't say anything.

"She'd been crossing those tracks for *years,* Mel."

"You really want to go back over this?"

"Over what? You mean do I not want to avoid this like at Christmas?"

"She wouldn't go and hurt us like that, okay?" Meryl shrugged. "She just wouldn't."

Their mother wouldn't have wanted to hurt them. But she also could seem entirely oblivious, especially when Vickie and Meryl were little, and she'd lose them shopping and every year at the hospital fair. She'd stride so far ahead, Vickie and Meryl would finally lose sight of her one bright note of color, a yellow scarf or red blouse. They'd sit on the pedestal of a mannequin, if they were at the mall, or by the cotton-candy machine at the fair until Lydia would finally appear, flushed with panic.

But when Lydia was crossing the tracks that day, maybe by the time she took into account the consequences of her disappearing from her daughters' lives, it was already too late for her to get out of the train's way.

"What if she didn't know what she was doing until the very last minute?" Vickie asked.

"*What?*"

"I mean, she wouldn't *plan* to hurt us. . . ."

"So you're thinking at the last possible second she decided, 'Gee, maybe I'll just throw myself in front of this train'?"

"Maybe that's exactly what she did," Vickie said, annoyed with Meryl for being so dismissive. "Maybe the only way she had the courage to do it in the first place was to *make* it into an accident—to not even admit it to herself."

"Is this something you want to believe, Vickie?"

"No. . . ."

"Then what difference does it make?" Meryl said with a tiredness that surprised Vickie. "What do you think it can change?"

Gazing at the collage of photographs, Vickie felt as estranged as when Meryl had given up trying to convince Vickie about the confirmation classes and gone back downstairs. Later, Vickie had found Meryl and their mother sitting on the counter licking cookie batter from a bowl and talking as easily as they could on rainy Sunday afternoons when they stayed in their nightgowns doing jigsaw puzzles together. When they could seem closer than Vickie and Meryl had ever been.

Glenn came in from the barn.

"What have you been doing all morning down there?" Meryl asked.

He looked at the newspapers spread across the kitchen. "You're painting the cabinets?"

"It's been over a month since you sanded them."

"You have to be at work soon."

"I wanted to at least start."

"So you think you can talk Ruth into letting you drive her T-bird?" Glenn asked, greeting Vickie as he always did, as if she'd never been away.

"Poor Glenn," Meryl said. "He's dying to take that car out."

"I wouldn't count on it," Vickie said. "She's prizing it like it's been in the family for generations."

"My father had a T-bird, but my parents almost split up over it. My mother hated that car—it was so 'impractical.' "

Glenn didn't seem rugged enough to be building a house; with his short-cropped hair and square-rimmed glasses, Vickie could more easily picture him behind a bank desk. He was good-looking in a way that had never appealed to her, like the men modeling faded dungaree styles in advertisements on the sides of New York buses. All the same, she'd always been fond of him, especially appreciative of the impartial view he tried to take whenever she and Meryl would nearly come to blows over Vickie's old boyfriend Kyle.

"How's the house coming?" Vickie asked.

"Getting down to the details," he said, taking a couple of lampshades from the shelf. "Meryl bugs me about this stuff, but I knew I'd be wanting these—they'll fit the fixtures I've put in, from the twenties, and from your dad's store, in fact."

"Then maybe we'll get our own house done," Meryl said. She pointed up at the loft, at the door that was to open onto a deck Glenn had yet to build. "I don't know how long we've had that dresser pushed up against there so the kids won't fall out."

"Well, the cabinets, anyway, I think could have waited."

"The paint was peeling off in sheets, Glenn."

He dusted off the shades with his shirttail. "This is some party she's throwing, isn't it?"

"Glenn thinks I'm getting carried away," Meryl said.

"Well, you are, aren't you?" He laughed.

"It's a *milestone*."

"You've invited the entire town, Mel."

"And it's easy for you to exaggerate since you're not doing a whole lot to help."

Vickie wasn't used to this kind of exchange between them, more used to how they'd always been a team, up on ladders together reshingling the roof. "I should get going."

"You just got here," Meryl said.

"I want to stop by Kyle's."

Meryl frowned, and Vickie hated how she could still disapprove of him.

"Sorry about the chickens," Vickie said, feeling like she should be apologizing for something more.

"I could kill that dog," Glenn said.

"Could you?"

He smiled. "Maybe."

CHAPTER 6

ERYL NEVER KNEW what exactly
was going on between her sister
and Kyle even though it had been
two years now since they broke up, and lately she'd
been convincing herself that there was nothing at all.
But it made her nervous now to think of Vickie over
at his place, and she listened for Daryll on his intercom, for that soothing rhythmic sound of his
breathing.

"I wish you'd be a little more supportive about
this party, at least in front of my sister."

"And I wish you wouldn't keep at me about the house," Glenn said.

Meryl cleared the table, knowing it would become cluttered again and with the most miscellaneous of things—Alex's plastic barrette bows, an empty stamp book, stray playing cards.

"It *is* just a party, Mel."

"Gramma deserves something special."

"You could have something special without renting out a hall."

"It's not out of your pocket—why are you worrying?"

"I know. It's out of your father's pocket."

"We're not even having it catered."

He didn't say anything.

"It's important to me, Glenn."

"I guess that's it—I don't really understand that, why it's so important."

Meryl didn't understand either, except that when she was planning the decorations, menu, and order of music, she'd felt invigorated in a way she hadn't since her mother died. As invigorated as when she used to clean the old house every spring and open wide all the windows.

"I mean, you've never been especially fond of Ruth, anyway," Glenn said. "Of course, you love her and all—"

"This party is *important* to me. Shouldn't that be enough, the mere fact that it's important to me?"

Meryl was surprised at the shakiness in her voice,
and she had to sit down.

She would have to sit down again and again, the
energy as suddenly sapped out of her as on that
morning three months after the funeral when her
skin took on the green pallor from the half moon of
stained glass above the bathroom mirror, and the
porcelain was cold as ice beneath her hands as she
leaned on the sink. She had to lower herself onto the
edge of the tub, a new loneliness settling into a dull
ache between her ribs.

That was the first time she'd fully grasped that
her mother was gone. That Lydia wouldn't be coming by to sit in a fold-up chair dangling her feet in
Daryll's baby pool, to snap off the wilted buds from
Meryl's violets, or to pick up the place as she never
did at the old house. And she wouldn't be coming
by to complain about Vickie after their weekly phone
call. "Dog training? She's going to train dogs?"
Lydia had wailed after Vickie told her she was giving
up photography. "All that time in high school I
couldn't get her *out* of the darkroom."

If it wasn't about Vickie, it was about Ruth leaving the French doors open so that the house filled
with flies, or about Blake giving too many little old
ladies discounts on repairs for their art deco lamps.
About them, Lydia would rattle on distractedly, digging her hand into Meryl's jar of yogurt-coated rai-

sins, and Meryl would rattle on in the same way, complaining about indecisive customers who would leave her with a tangled pile of frames to be rehung. Perhaps that's what Meryl missed most, how she and her mother never had to talk about anything in particular. How they could simply be together.

Glenn came over and massaged her shoulders, seeming to understand as instinctively as on that morning when he'd found her sitting on the edge of the tub. She closed her eyes and leaned back against him, feeling the tension leaving her shoulders.

She didn't know why Vickie had to be going back over the accident, although it was just like her to attempt to puzzle out the unanswerable. At dinner she used to ask questions like "How can a star blink more than a million times a second?" Their parents had appreciated Meryl's more school-related questions whose answers could be looked up in the encyclopedia.

Meryl reached for Glenn's hands. "Vickie thinks it wasn't until the last second she knew what she was doing crossing the tracks."

He was quiet for a moment before saying, "Well, that maybe sounds like your mother. Remember when she tore down all that lattice? It wasn't until it was too late that she thought to ask me if it could be repaired."

"We're not talking about lattice."

"I'm only saying that your mother was hard to read—I don't even know what she thought of *me*."

"She adored you, you know that, especially since you refused to marry me until you could afford a down payment."

"She didn't adore me; she tolerated me. I didn't even belong to the club."

Not only didn't Glenn belong to the club, but neither had he gone to the private school. He went to the public school in Sladebrook, and Meryl had met him one afternoon at the mall there in the video arcade.

"She wasn't as superficial as that," she said.

"I know she wasn't. She just pretended to be. That's what I mean: she was hard to read."

The fact was, Lydia had been able to seem particularly frivolous, and Meryl was sorry her senior year in high school when she'd convinced Glenn into going to the club's annual ball; they had to wait for Lydia while she repeatedly put up her hair only to take it down again, until Ruth finally stomped up the stairs and gave her a three-minute warning. "You'd think this was her prom," Glenn had said amusedly.

It was a nervousness Meryl didn't often see in her mother, but Lydia had fussed so every year. At age seven, Meryl remembered admiring how swiftly her mother could swirl up her hair, but then she'd be taking it all down again, the pins clattering so noisily into the bathroom sink Meryl was sure their glass heads would shatter. When Ruth would finally come upstairs with her warning, Lydia would pin her hair up any old way. Meryl couldn't bear seeing her struggle so, and she'd take the pins to try swirling it up herself. Lydia would seem grateful, sitting hunkered on the toilet so that her daughter could reach.

Alex came in and ran to Glenn, raising her arms to be picked up.

"You're getting too big for this, Pumpkin," he said, lifting her.

"Aunt Vickie said I can visit her in New York."

"At the rate she's going, she won't be able to *afford* New York," Meryl said.

"She said she'd take me to a ball game."

"Maybe you'll get lucky and they'll hit a foul ball into your row," Glenn said.

"I told her we'll see," Meryl said, although Glenn and Alex seemed too absorbed in each other to hear her. At bedtime, it was her father whom Alex preferred having read to her since he'd act out her favorite jungle stories. When Meryl peeked in, Glenn would be crawling around with a Halloween plastic wand for a bone in his mouth. Alex, in a fit of giggles on the bed, would not even notice her mother, and Meryl would quietly close the door. She would go check on Daryll, and if he was awake, he'd reach up his hands and she'd cup them as if catching butterflies.

"I thought Vickie had gotten work," Glenn said, lowering Alex. She clung to his leg until she saw her pink box where she'd left her bones spread out on the couch.

"Freelance work—that's hardly secure."

He cut off what was left on the chicken carcass from Meryl's last batch of soup for his lunch. "Well, she's pretty self-sufficient."

"Self-destructive is more like it—every time I turn around, she's wreaking havoc on her life."

"To you it's havoc; to her maybe it's sensible."

"Sensible? What has she ever done that was sensible? She's still blundering around like she's eighteen and running off to the desert again."

"Mel . . . You can sound like a little old hen, worse than your mother."

She felt all the tension returning to her shoulders. "My *mother* took up smoking again when Vickie was away those months, when she couldn't even drop a postcard letting us know she was all right."

Glenn glanced over at Alex where she was carefully packing up her bones. She'd grown so quiet, Meryl thought she'd gone back to her room.

Lowering her voice, Meryl said, "I just wish she hadn't let Ted go. He was so . . . *good* to her, you know? But she has trouble with that, anyone who wants to treat her right."

"You never met him; how do you know he was good to her?"

"I don't, I guess, but from what she's told me I know he wasn't enough of a risk. She's always preferred that anyway, crossing a precipice when she could more safely walk around it."

Frowning, Glenn packed his chicken sandwich into Alex's old Snow White lunch box.

Meryl knew that Glenn thought she was too protective of Vickie and perhaps she was, but only because old habits were hard to break—Meryl couldn't remember not looking out for her sister, from the time when their mother allowed Meryl to help sponge her in the kitchen sink. Meryl was five then and she'd felt such pride, a pride that had less to do with Vickie than with the fact that their mother was entrusting the baby to her as she wouldn't even entrust those silver cups Meryl liked to reach for in the buffet.

The way Vickie lived her life so haphazardly, she could seem as vulnerable now as she did then when sometimes Meryl would examine her carefully, brushing her lashes so that her eyelids fluttered and staring down her throat to her tiny pink tonsils. Later, Meryl would see her out in the yard nestling clumps of hair from her brush into the snowball bush for the birds, and she'd be reminded of how Vickie could sit alone like that, waiting for her after school,

tying an old lunch straw into an elaborate knot.
Meryl would go outside, but Vickie would wander
off to be by herself anyway, and Meryl would be
left weaving a limp wreath of dandelions.

Vickie had been getting up and wandering away
from her since she was learning to walk and would
struggle against Meryl when she was only trying to
keep her little sister from plunging into the coffee
table. As if, even back then, Vickie could only prove
herself by plunging forward alone.

Of course, what right did Meryl have now to be
judging her sister when she herself was taking risks
she'd never thought Vickie even capable of? She listened for Daryll on the intercom and longed for him
to awaken, one of her favorite moments when he'd
look for her around the corner of his crib.

"I better get going," Glenn said.

"Don't forget the coffee urns."

"Oh, damn."

"I can't do it, Glenn. I've got to get the kids over
to Gail's." Gail had been Lydia's best friend and was
now the one who watched the kids while Meryl was
at work.

"And I have to return all that warped
lumber."

"I told the church office you'd be by this afternoon—they're nice enough to be lending them in
the first place."

"They'll understand if I pick them up in the morning."

Meryl rummaged through a kitchen drawer for the aspirin, expecting to find the bottle mixed in among the baby-food jars of tacks, rubber bands, and twisters. Every time she tried to organize things, they rarely wound up back where they belonged. "This is exactly what I didn't want to have happen, leaving things to the last minute."

"You have two whole days yet, and you've been preparing for this thing for weeks already. You're even finding time to paint the cabinets."

"Well, if I didn't, who would?"

He put on his cap, carefully adjusting the visor.

"Anyway, that's not really the point, is it?" Meryl said. "It's not time we're talking about."

"All right."

"Never mind."

"Do you want me to get them or not?" Glenn snapped. "What *is* your point here?"

"I've got to be going now," Alex announced.

Meryl wondered at this new talent her daughter had developed of growing so quiet. Meryl was sure she had left the room.

"You can't, Alex," Meryl said. "I've got to get you over to Gail's soon."

"I won't go far."

"You just got back. You don't need to go off again."

"Oh, let her *go,*" Glenn said.

Meryl hammered the lid onto the paint can. Alex left, and in a moment Meryl heard the rattle of her bike chain down the driveway.

"Look, I have to get over to the hardware store sometime and it's in that direction," Glenn said. "So I might as well do it today."

"It's all right, I can do it. I'll just get going sooner."

Meryl thought he'd insist, but he only said, "I may be a little late tonight if I don't get that tiling finished."

"I'm going out, remember," she said.

"You just went out a couple of nights ago."

"That was for Lisa's birthday."

Glenn didn't say anything, grabbing the frosted shades and his lunch box.

"I don't give you a hard time about your nights out," Meryl said.

"Yeah, but I'm not the one making excuses to be out every other night."

"Excuses?"

He let the screen door slam behind him.

She strained to hear the last note of the familiar knock of his truck, feeling the distance between them. Some nights when he came home late from work, she'd already be in bed, but she'd lie awake listening for the canned laughter from some television program he'd turn on in the living room. The laughter was so small and tinny, it could have been rising from some great depth. Some depth she could actually look down into, like the old well in Ruth's backyard, into which she used to drop beads so she could hear them ping like final weak calls.

Eventually the television would be turned off, and she'd hear him taking a shower. The other night, he came in wrapped in a towel and sat on the edge of their bed. Taking off his glasses, he dangled them between his knees as he stared at the floor, and Meryl had felt suddenly terribly sorry. She ran her hand down his back until he got into bed. They felt for each other until she got on top and rocking gently, framed his face with her hands.

"That was nice," he whispered afterward, and she knew he meant it was nice for her to have been the one to make the first move, something she hadn't done for the past few months.

They lay in their favorite position, facing each other with their legs intertwined and Glenn's hands nestled between her breasts. His hands finally went limp and Meryl knew he was asleep. She got up.

She sat out on the back stoop. The sky shone icily in the mirrors propped up against the house, and that old ache throbbed between her ribs. An ache that no longer came and went only when she was especially missing her mother, when she'd imagine hearing the train before it was scheduled to pass through, as sometimes she imagined she could hear the surf slamming against the beach when it was only a north wind. It was an ache now that could come and go when she wasn't thinking about her mother at all. She leaned her head on her arms.

"What is it?" Glenn asked, suddenly there behind her.

"Nothing," she said.

"It's not nothing."

She didn't say anything else, but she thought he'd sit with her; those first months after her mother died, he'd sit with her on the couch when he found her up crying. He'd never found her sitting outside before. And she wasn't crying.

He went back to bed, and she wondered if this time he could feel how much she didn't want him touching her.

She could no longer hear Glenn's truck, and she felt as if she were falling from some great height. Her palms began to sweat and her face grew clammy. She'd developed a fear of heights sometime within the first few years after they were married, when she no longer could conceive of getting up on a ladder to help Glenn reshingle the roof.

She heard the sticky steps of Daryll shuffling in his feet pajamas and she landed abruptly.

"How did you do it? How'd you get out?"

He grinned, bending over into his favorite posture so that he could stare at her through his legs, obviously pleased with his new trick. No matter how high she raised the railings, he was able to climb out of his crib, and she wondered that he never hurt himself.

CHAPTER 7

ERYL THINKS I've lost control of my life," Vickie said, sitting on the overturned horse trough she and Kyle sometimes used as a hot tub. Propping it up on bricks, Kyle would build a fire under it and they'd sit opposite each other with a bottle of wine and glasses set up on a board between them.

"Well, have you?" he asked, tossing a root into a tangled pile on the edge of his yard. He was preparing an organic garden by first planting buckwheat, he'd explained, as a kind of fertilizer.

"Around her, I have." She'd left Meryl's feeling as she used to, coming home with scraped knees from trying to crawl through the large drainage pipe beneath Atlas Road. Meryl would clean her up before her mother could ask where she'd been.

"I quit my job," Vickie said.

"Really, you quit? Well, you've always been like this, moving on to the next thing."

"That was exactly her point. Maybe that's the only reason I do it, anyway, always to be moving. The great unknown. The big black hole."

"Personally, I think you're afraid to succeed."

"You're analyzing me now?"

"Why else would you give up a position you've worked four years toward? It's like your photography."

"I got sick of doing pretty linen place settings."

"You didn't have to go and give it up entirely. You could have gone back to what you were doing in high school, jumping up somewhere, catching some weird angle."

"Remember the pictures I took of you in here?" she asked, rapping her knuckles against the tub. "I liked *those* angles."

"Seriously. You were good."

"I was good because you thought I was good."

Kyle himself was a photographer, and Vickie never would have pursued photography if he hadn't believed so in her. No one in her family had been particularly encouraging, except for her father who helped set up a darkroom in the basement.

"The trick is to fool the bugs," Kyle said.

"Bugs can be fooled?"

"You mix up the vegetables, like planting a ring of corn around the cabbages, something that helps keep out the rabbits, too. And most insects hate scallions, so I'm planting those among the radishes."

"Sounds complicated."

"And expensive. It cost me almost a thousand just to get this tilled."

Vickie liked to look at him. Except for wrinkles that had deepened around his eyes, he didn't seem much older than when she first met him eleven years ago, when he was thirty and she was sixteen. He had always seemed tall to her even though he was actually quite short, with a broad chest and a head of thick black curls. He was part Greek on his mother's side, and when they were still together, he'd promised to take her to the Peloponnesus where his great-great-grandmother had lived, selling roasted peppers.

Although Kyle didn't lack for commissions photographing weddings and receptions and covering events for the local newspaper, he preferred living meagerly. His apartment was above an abandoned gas station, and he subsisted mostly on bruised vegetables and fruit from the bins behind the A&P, and on fish he'd catch out in the old, peeling rowboat he kept overturned on the side of the garage. Occasionally he'd find a deer freshly run down on a back road and skin it to keep in his freezer all winter.

"I should be planting already, but I've been over at my father's too much, trying to get that place in shape. He wants to up the rent, but I talked him out of it. He'd have to make some improvements first and he's too cheap for that. The kitchen floor is buckling, and every summer I have to replace the freezer tube in that ancient refrigerator."

Kyle's father had retired from his landscaping business and moved to Chicago to be closer to his other son's children after Kyle's mother died six years ago.

"Why doesn't he just sell it?" Vickie asked.

"He's hoping I'll want it, I guess, still expecting me to settle down one day."

She laughed. "Right." She could no more imagine Kyle settling down than she could his giving up his passion for those things he could only do alone, like playing the saxophone he'd taught himself.

"I know. But sometimes I wonder," he said, lifting her off the tub. "Like what would I do if a meteor fell in my yard."

"A meteor?"

"It happened to this guy on the news." He smoothed back her hair from her forehead. "A meteor burned a hole right through the hood of his car,

71

then blasted a two-foot hole in the ground. This piece of rock had traveled how many hundreds of thousands of miles? And there he is, holding it in his hands."

"What does this have to do with settling down?"

"Nothing, really. Except he didn't know what he had in his hands. They asked him what he was going to do with it, and he talked about keeping it on his coffee table. On his goddamn *coffee table*. I don't know, sometimes, I guess, I'm just feeling like I'm going through the motions. A meteor could fall right in my own yard, and I wouldn't know what hit me." He rocked her side to side. "I miss you, Vickie."

"You do, huh?"

"You do too," he said, gently hooking her ankle with one foot so that they fell together. He pulled her on top of him, running his hands down around her buttocks. "You miss me too."

She felt herself opening up, wanting him. She did miss him. And she missed this, their spontaneity together. She hadn't been able to reach that level of intimacy with anyone else, where they could forget themselves to the point of silliness. It didn't take being drunk or Halloween for them to run outside naked except for bed sheets draped over their heads. And one summer, they made the ugliest kite they could imagine, a cow with large droopy udders whose picture wound up in the *Lawton Gazette*. They could spend entire afternoons making fun of ceramic ballerinas and polyester shirts advertised on the cable home-shopping channel, and they both had an insatiable appetite for books about the brain, often trading trivia about REM sleep and neurotransmitters. They liked best trying to "unbaffle the baffable," to answer questions Vickie still would ask herself, like how a star could blink more than a million times a second.

"I want you," Glenn said.

Vickie slid her hands into his jeans. "You can have me."

"You know what I mean. Don't you ever think about that? Where we might be now if we were still together?"

When she didn't answer, he said, "Hypothetically, of course. Like what if a meteor fell in your yard."

In the two years since they broke up, this was the first time either had mentioned getting back together. She was the one to break up with him. She could never return to live here, to this town that would always feel too small, and she thought Kyle had understood, since neither could his lifestyle ever be suited to city living.

But occasionally they'd lapse into the old ways, heating up the hot tub or making love in his van parked at the beach when they'd meant only to go fishing. Back in his apartment after making love, she'd lie with her back to him as she gazed at his lamp with the magazine reproductions of Matisse nudes he'd slipped between the shade's sheets of glass, and he would run his hands down her side. He'd pause in his favorite spot, the "deep valley" of her waist, and she'd feel how he could still make her feel—as delicate and alluring as she'd ever imagined only Meryl could feel.

"Oh, we'd be right here," Kyle said. "Huddled with kids around those old gas pumps. And you'd be working at Cray's Deli serving stale doughnuts."

"You don't like kids."

"That's not it—I like kids. I didn't think I'd have the patience. Maybe with my own I would." He laughed. "Oh I don't know, I'm obviously thinking too much lately—I'll be over cleaning up after the last tenants and find some kid's toy and wonder what I'm doing there, cleaning up after someone else's life."

She wasn't used to such restlessness in Kyle. What she'd admired most about him was how content he'd always been with his own aloneless, and she was disappointed.

"So you don't think about it?" he asked.

"I don't know that I . . . see it."

He only nodded.

"I can't move back here, Kyle."

"I know. That's why I said 'hypothetically.' I mean, what are the chances of a meteor falling, anyway?" He looked at the sky. "The light is right now."

"For crabbing?"

"Come with me?"

After this, she thought maybe she shouldn't, but she didn't want to leave. She wondered when she'd ever be able to stop that, wanting so much to be with him.

The first time Vickie saw Kyle, he was crabbing at the bay. He finally noticed her watching him from her favorite rock where she liked to sit and read after school, and as an excuse to talk to him, she asked if she could see the crabs in his pail. She hadn't known what exactly to make of him. While she could tell by his weathered hands that he was at least in his thirties, he had the pent-up energy of a boy, playfully romping down the beach to scare the seagulls away from his pail.

But there had been that aloneness about him, in the way he'd pulled aside the grasses to show her a nest of baby horseshoe crabs and held a scallop beneath the water so she could see how its row of blue eyes glittered like jewels. It was an aloneness she would see again when he'd examine the jacks ball he usually carried around in his pocket, in the way he could become lost in its pattern of sequins. An aloneness she understood.

No one in her family had been able to see what

she saw in him, least of all her mother. "You didn't tell me he was twice your age," Lydia had said after first meeting him. He'd given her a basket of peaches he'd picked himself, but she'd been skeptical of peaches growing in Massachusetts.

"I didn't think it was important," Vickie said.

"Of *course* it's important when you're only sixteen."

They were in the living room, and her father was sitting on the piano bench, straightening the magazines. Whenever Vickie and her mother began like this, he'd begin straightening things.

Lydia had been sitting in the velvet chair, but she got up to run her fingers across the radiators, saying, "Look, honey. You can't blame us for being a little concerned. . . . We don't know him."

"You can get to know him."

Her mother examined the dust on her fingertips. "Maybe so. But I can't help not liking your disappearing with him, when we don't know where you are."

"We can't forbid her to see him, Lydia," Blake said. "She's going to see him anyway."

Lydia shook her head sadly. "You will, won't you?"

Vickie leaned against the French doors, wishing she could be outside. Wishing she was little again so she could sprint across the yard.

Her mother sighed, sitting back in the chair. "Well, if you're going to see him, then you can see him here."

"Here?"

"And you're not to go to your room with him."

"Can't you *try* trusting me?"

"It's not you, Vickie, it's him," her father said, one hand resting on his tidy pile of magazines. "We don't know that we can trust him."

Vickie and Kyle would sit out behind the maple tree, out of sight of Vickie's mother who periodically checked on them through the French doors. Lydia would then begin weeding her flower garden, weeding until there was nothing left to weed and she'd exclaim when she accidently pulled up a daisy. Vickie and Kyle would move into the living room, and soon afterward Lydia would be sorting through the junk mail thrown into the large china bowl on the hall table, a task she otherwise left to Ruth.

"I feel like I'm dating for the first time in junior high," Kyle whispered one afternoon when they were sitting in there. But as long as it meant he could keep seeing Vickie, Kyle would continue coming over. He told her again and again that he didn't want to lose her, and neither did he want to displease her parents.

It was Vickie's idea to start lying to her mother. She told her she'd joined the theater club and had to stay for rehearsals after school when she was really meeting Kyle.

"I found a whole mess of blue crabs here last month," Kyle said. "You should have seen these blues—they had these little eggs attached to their asses. I tried picking only those without eggs but when I opened them up, they had eggs inside." From the back of his van, he took out the inner tube and the old vegetable basket he used to collect the crabs. "Hopefully, they're done spawning by now."

When Vickie had last gone crabbing with him, they'd found nothing but spider crabs. They'd steamed them anyway, to suck out whatever little meat there was in the legs.

"Ruth invited me to her party," Kyle said.

"Did she?" Vickie laughed.

Ruth would never admit to liking Kyle, not so much because he wasn't of her social milieu, she'd explained, but because she thought him a little "strange." But Vickie knew she'd always been curious about him. "It's surprising he doesn't poison us all," she'd ruminated once when he was over for dinner and picked her some blackberries from their own woods to serve with the ice cream for dessert.

"You're going, I hope," Vickie said.

"You want me to?"

"It would be the first time anyone in my family actually acknowledged you."

"I don't know . . ."

"It sounds like it's going to be a mob scene anyway. You'll blend right in."

He laughed. "Your mother would go gray."

"Well, that's hardly something you have to worry about now, is it?"

"Sorry, sweetie."

She watched as he tied one end of a rope around the inner tube—the other end to be tied around his waist—and nestled the basket into the tube. "I know. I've just been thinking about her. I've been thinking maybe she did kill herself."

He was quiet for a moment, in that thoughtful way he had when he wanted to say the right thing. "Well, I guess it's hard to accept that someone could die as suddenly as that. You have to rationalize it some way."

"Is that what I'm doing? Rationalizing it?"

"Why are you thinking about it then?"

"That's what Meryl wanted to know."

"Just don't start torturing yourself, okay? I know how you can punish yourself."

"Punish myself? For what?"

"I don't know. You tell me."

She didn't know that she was punishing herself, although there were moments when she'd feel traces of shame, even on the way to the memorial service. She'd been the one to hold her mother's ashes while her father drove and her grandmother stared stolidly out the window. Unable to choose an urn, they'd all settled for the crematorium's tin can, and Vickie couldn't resist peeking inside—she wanted to feel whether the ashes were soft as powder, but they were tightly sealed in a plastic bag.

Kyle handed her a snorkel and mask. "Did you know crabs actually can put their adolescence on hold? If conditions are right, they can stop their growth up to something like three months. And when the female's shell is soft, the male takes hold of her, protects her like that."

"That's sweet."

He smiled. "When she's real soft, he fucks her."

"That's better than sweet." She wrapped her arms around him as he was getting the nets out of the van.

"What are you up to, Firecracker?"

"Nothing really new."

He laughed, gently unclasping her arms. He'd never pulled away from her before.

"What is it?"

"What is what?"

"Are you seeing someone, Kyle?"

"Not exactly."

"Not exactly?"

He tested the temperature of the water, then went back for the wet suits. "We both just don't want to be alone now."

She gazed at him for a long moment, at the way

he shook out the wet suits so that they made a flap-
ping sound like sails. "You were the one talking
about getting back together."

"And you were the one who said you couldn't
see it."

Since they'd broken up, as far as she knew, he'd
gone out with only a couple of women, and only
briefly. She realized now that she hadn't expected
this, that he would actually become involved with
someone else. Maybe because she'd somehow
known all along that he would always want them
to get back together.

Handing her a pair of flippers, he said, "Try not
to kick up the bottom."

CHAPTER 8

"YOU SHOULDN'T leave the door open like that," Meryl said to Gail, finding her in her sewing room. Unlike Ruth's house, Gail's was devoid of any family history, furnished with Ethan Allen loveseats and plastic flowers. Everything was in pairs, with the mantel framed by two brass candlesticks and a couple of sunburst pillows tucked into either end of the love seats. Whatever tables there were had a pair of bookends less to show off the few old *Reader's Digest*s than the bookends—two frogs, two doves, two wooden fishermen.

Gail had always sewed, and after her divorce twelve years ago, she began her own small upholstery business by advertising locally in the *Lawton Gazette* and posting flyers at the A&P.

"Well, I knew it would be only you," Gail said.

"It could have been anyone."

"Hey, kiddos," Gail said, flinging back her auburn braid with quite a flourish, her hazel eyes widening. Although her hair had begun to gray, she could still seem girlish.

Since Lydia had been the one to watch the kids while Meryl was at work, Meryl had tried for a while leaving them with her grandmother. But once when she was picking them up, Ruth was so bent on finding her letter opener she'd forgotten Alex was playing on the third floor. Blake was better at keeping track of them if he was home, but he'd allow them down in the basement, and Meryl could imagine Daryll piercing himself with an awl.

"The dogs out back?" Alex asked.

"They've been asking when you'd be by," Gail said.

Alex grinned, dipping her hand into Gail's old teapot of buttons to let them run out between her fingers. Meryl couldn't get over how Alex seemed to adore Gail as much as she had adored her own grandmother. Lydia would play her favorite games, Twister and hide-and-seek, while Gail rarely played with either of them, although she'd repainted her son's old sandbox for Daryll and replaced the rope on the tire swing for Alex. But Meryl was confident she kept a good eye on them; stitching some arm cover or headrest, she would work outside while they played in the yard.

"You're a little ahead of things, aren't you?" Gail asked, glancing at her watch.

"Hope it's all right. I have to stop and pick up the coffee urns from the church before work."

"I could do that, Mel."

"Oh, you've got the kids—that's plenty."

"We can stop for strudel afterward at the cafe."

"Yeah! Let her take us, Mommy," Alex said, scooping out more buttons. "Let her get the urns. The urns, the urns, the stupid *urns*."

Meryl looked at her impatiently, and Alex left the room, saying, "I'm gonna say hi to the dogs." She skipped down the hall, singing, "To Mindy, to Clara and Sage. Mindy, Clara, *Sage!*"

Daryll was squirming to get down but Meryl didn't allow him in Gail's sewing room, afraid he'd swallow a button or maybe even a pin. "Well, thanks. And thanks for being the only one who's not treating me like I'm nuts for throwing this party in the first place."

"Why would you be nuts?"

"I don't know, ask Glenn, or now Vickie—"

"Vickie? How is she? I'll have to stop by later."

"She's quit her job."

"Oh. Well . . ."

"Why am I the only one concerned?"

"Of course you're concerned, she's your baby sister. Anyway, a party might just be what we all need." Gail squinted at the late-morning sun as if it hurt her eyes, saying, "I mean, it's practically summer, for goodness' sake."

Meryl knew what she meant, that the air had grown warm and sweetly scented, but it felt as gray and cold as if the ground were still frozen. She'd never understood exactly what had made Gail and her mother such good friends, and she'd never been particularly comfortable around Gail herself. But she found some solace in being around her now if only because they both couldn't shake that, the chill of winter.

"So now you have time for coffee before you run off," Gail said.

"A little time . . . ," Meryl said, following her into the kitchen.

Gail and her mother might never have been friends at all if they hadn't been neighbors; people like Gail's husband worked for people like Ruth cleaning out chimneys or repairing hot-water boilers. They met one afternoon around Christmas, in the woods between their two streets, when Lydia was collecting pinecones for the mantel and Gail was looking for her son, Ray, who built forts out there of old tires and rotting logs.

Soon afterward, Gail asked them all over for dinner, and she set a table of rose-tinted glass dishes. Periodically, she would get up to refill their already full water glasses as Meryl had seen only waitresses do. Meryl was trying to hook her thumbs through the scalloped edge of the tablecloth when Gail's husband, Jeffrey, began apologizing for the slightly overdone steak.

"She must not have been paying attention," he said.

"How could she with you hollering for more chips every five minutes?" Ray said.

Jeffrey glared at his son.

Beginning to slouch, Ray said, "You just could get it yourself, I think, once in a while."

"Please, you two . . . ," Gail whispered, and Jeffrey threw his rose-tinted wineglass at the wall.

Ruth liked to tell and retell the story of that dinner to the family as if they hadn't all been there themselves. ". . . and he threw his glass at the *wall*."

Lydia would have no comment, since she and Gail continued to see each other. Often in the mornings Gail would drop by for breakfast, and when Vickie and Meryl were leaving for school, she'd already have poured her own coffee, taken off the same worn moccasins she usually wore, and settled herself at the kitchen table.

When Meryl was home sick one day, she heard Gail and her mother laughing in the kitchen after Ruth had left for her weekly bridge game and luncheon at the club. Meryl went downstairs pretending she wanted more juice.

The table was still littered with toast crusts even though it was almost lunchtime. They both smoked back then, and Gail flicked her ashes into her empty coffee cup. Around her own house, she kept conveniently located ashtrays in the shape of turtles lying on their backs, and the night of that dinner, she'd emptied them as periodically as she'd filled their water glasses.

Gail had taken off her moccasins and she sat with one leg tucked under her so that her skirt was hitched up. Meryl could see a mole on her inner thigh and couldn't imagine she was the same person who'd served them steak garnished with parsley on rose-tinted plates. They didn't notice Meryl as she went over to the refrigerator.

"Sprinkler systems. Can you imagine, going on for a good forty-five minutes about a sprinkler?" Lydia was saying. "Even for Mr. Olson."

Mr. Olson was a member of the club, and the night before had been the annual planning committee dinner.

"Well, you know those systems can be quite

sophisticated these days," Gail said. "Think of all the ramifications." Gail didn't belong to the country club and would openly make fun of its "archaic rituals."

Laughing so hard now, Lydia wiped her eyes on her napkin. "And that's what Mother said. I'm sitting there thinking this is the most inane conversation I've ever heard—and I've heard plenty—and there's Mother saying, 'Well, that's some system, isn't it? All those knobs and all.' When we came home, I said, 'Mother, he talked about sprinklers for *forty-five* minutes.' And she said, 'It's just small talk, dear. What's wrong with a little small talk?' " Lydia flicked her ashes into her own coffee cup. "I should have said, the problem is, small talk can make you as constipated as a bag of prunes."

Meryl had never heard her talk like that. She thought of all the time her mother could spend fretting about her hair for those club dances, and she slammed the refrigerator shut so her mother would stop laughing.

"What is it, honey? What do you need?" Lydia asked, abruptly getting up and piling the plates into the sink as if it was actually Ruth who'd overheard them. "Come here a minute, let me feel your head."

Lydia had been taking her temperature every hour, less able to keep collected over a common cold than real emergencies. When Meryl was bitten by a dog, she'd tied a tourniquet of dish towels around her wrist as if arranging a corsage.

"You'd think she had the plague," Gail said. She'd been the one to suggest a cup of honeyed tea to help soothe Meryl's sore throat.

"Don't tell me *I'm* neurotic," Lydia said. "You're the one who has to pull out the feather duster every time you come by."

"Honey, this place hasn't been dusted since the last generation," Gail said, getting up for a clean mug to pour herself more coffee. "Or however many generations have been in this house."

She opened a cabinet and took out a box of granola bars, and it bothered Meryl then how well she knew her way around their kitchen. For the first time, she noticed that Gail had hammertoes, probably the reason why she always wore those same cracked, worn moccasins.

One morning, Gail came in and sat at the table without even pouring herself coffee. Shakily, she lit a cigarette.

Lydia was finishing packing Meryl's and Vickie's lunches when she looked at Gail. "My God."

Gail's collar had fallen a little open, and Gail moved her hand to her neck, but not before Meryl, too, could glimpse the bruises there.

Lydia ripped open the buttons. Gail's whole chest was bruised. "Damn it, Gail."

"I'm all right."

"He's too much now, don't you see that? Don't you *see* that?"

"Lydia, the kids . . ."

Lydia quickly handed them their lunch boxes, saying, "Go on. It's all right. Go on to school."

It wasn't until eight years later that Gail finally divorced Jeffrey, after he smashed their son's fish tank and pushed Gail into the broken glass. Gail streaked up through the woods in only her night-gown and collapsed on Ruth's lawn. Meryl and Vickie watched from the hall window as their mother ran out to her. Gail held up her open hands as if in an offering, but in the light from the back porch, Meryl could see that they were bleeding. Her mother pressed her own nightgown into Gail's palms.

From Gail's kitchen window, Meryl watched Alex playing with the dogs. Meryl herself didn't like the dogs, especially the Lab, Clara, who'd jump up and try to lick her face. That time she was bitten she had to get twenty-four stitches, and since then she'd never quite overcome her fear of dogs.

The Lab tackled Alex to the ground, licking her face, and Meryl couldn't help asking, "You sure they won't get too overexcited?"

"They're gentle as rabbits," Gail said.

It was hard to believe Gail had actually adopted

the dogs in the first place, and such an unlikely trio—a Lab, an Irish setter, and a cocker spaniel. Meryl remembered Gail hadn't allowed her son any pets except for the fish, not with her shiny wood floors that her husband had varnished himself.

Alex nuzzled her face into the Lab's belly. "She really loves them, doesn't she," Meryl said.

"I know. And I should have gotten them long ago, when Ray wanted a dog." Gail carried the tray of coffee out to the table in the living-room alcove. "Speaking of, he called last night—he's been promoted to office manager. It's only Howard Johnson's but it's his first real job."

"That's great," Meryl said, never having been much interested in Ray partly because he was already in high school when Meryl was only beginning fifth grade and partly because he spent most of his time hooked up to his headphones surrounded by a sea of albums. It was shortly after the fish tank incident that he moved to Texas.

"It is great, for him," Gail said. "The way he's never been able to hold down anything for very long."

"Sounds like Vickie."

"Oh, Vickie's not like that, Mel—Vickie's not lazy. A little indecisive, perhaps, but not lazy."

Gail had always been especially sympathetic toward Vickie, too much so, Meryl thought, remembering the time Gail helped Vickie hide a turtle after their mother insisted she return it to its "natural habitat." Gail wrapped it in a soaked washcloth so Vickie could take it to school, and it was Ruth who noticed her school bag leaking.

"Anything else I can do?" Gail asked.

"You're making those casseroles, that's plenty. And you're picking up the coffee urns," Meryl said. "Something Glenn was supposed to do but now says he can't."

Gail looked at her carefully.

"He just has all this warped lumber to return."

"Are you two okay?"

"We're fine," Meryl said, trying to sound casual.

"I just wondered if something's been going on."

"Like what? You haven't been around us. I mean, us together, not lately, anyway. . . ."

"I've been around you."

Meryl's hands began to sweat, and she felt her face growing clammy as if again she were looking down from some great height. "We're having a few financial pressures, that's all."

"There's Ruth, isn't there? If you're in a real bind?"

"We're not in a real bind, just . . . in between things."

"So you're all right?"

"We're *fine*."

Gail nodded, looking injured as she skimmed some invisible sediment from the surface of her cof-

fee, but Meryl couldn't help resenting her for trying
to fill the space left by her mother.

The fact was, Meryl couldn't have told her own
mother about what was actually going on, let alone
Gail. Reminded of that, she felt that old ache between her ribs return, and she looked out at her
daughter. Alex had pillowed her head against the
Lab, and they both lay stretched out in the sun.

CHAPTER 9

I HEAR YOU'VE actually invited Kyle."
Vickie was helping Ruth polish the good
serving spoons for dinner. Ruth's son, Warren, and his family were expected to arrive that
afternoon.

"Oh, well . . . I ran into him," Ruth said, holding
up the wineglasses to the light and placing the ones
to be washed on a tray. She had on what she would
wear to clean, a terry-cloth robe that hung as loosely
as a choir gown. "It was the polite thing to do.
You're streaking the handles."

Ruth rarely pulled out those good spoons except at Easter and Christmas. "Why are you going to all this trouble just for Uncle Warren? We're only having a barbecue," Vickie asked.

"I'm not doing this for Warren; I'm doing it for Anna. When we visit them, she always makes such an effort, is so thoughtful."

"Too thoughtful," Vickie said.

"Your aunt Anna is a sweet, good woman."

"I didn't say she wasn't. She just seems always to be trying to impress us."

It wasn't only at Christmas when Aunt Anna brought elaborately wrapped gifts with fancy tags, but every time they visited. And she had this way of perching on the edge of her seat as Vickie imagined she must have the time Uncle Warren brought her home to meet his mother.

"And I'm doing it for Shawna," Ruth said, adjusting the dish towel patterned with holly leaves she'd safety-pinned around her head. "Shawna who's so good about sending me pictures of Gordon. You should see the latest. Well, I don't know where they are, but Gordon's sitting on his Big Wheel. . . . It's precious."

Shawna was the exemplary grandchild. Not only did she faithfully send photographs, but she even remembered to send Ruth a card on Grandparents' Day.

Blake came into the dining room, and from the

wood shavings clinging to his flannel shirt Vickie knew he'd been working on his toy carvings in the basement. Some of the toys he'd sold to a store in town, mostly from his animated series of clothespin clowns that somersaulted when squeezed between two handles, string-operated firemen that climbed ropes, and Vickie's favorites, donkeys and roosters with moving heads and tails.

"What do you think?" he asked, placing a miniature cradle in Vickie's palm. He made miniature models of most toys before embarking on the actual pieces. "I'm thinking of a series fitting one within the other."

Vickie held the cradle at eye level.

"Blake, you were going to clean out that shed," Ruth said. "There won't be time later."

"You're right, Warren will look in there, too," Blake said. "Well, they'll be late anyhow. They're always late."

"That's hardly fair."

"Last time, you had to keep the pot roast warm until it turned to leather."

Ruth shook out the tablecloth and examined it for stains. "His life is hectic."

"Too hectic to attend his own sister's funeral," Vickie said.

Ruth dropped the cloth into a rumpled pile on the table. She picked up the tray of dirty glasses. "My son couldn't help that. He was overseas." Before Vickie could answer, the kitchen door was swinging shut behind her.

Vickie handed the cradle back to her father. "She makes it sound like he was at war."

Uncle Warren had been vacationing in New Zealand and claimed he and Anna couldn't get a flight back in time. He tried to atone for showing up five days late by challenging the funeral director about the bill. Although they had had the simplest of burials, they'd been charged as much as what other funeral parlors charged for a gold-plated urn and a private viewing. Anna had presented them with an enormous basket of fruit with the tag "Accept our condolences."

Perhaps Uncle Warren really couldn't have made it back in time, but it was just like Ruth to take that excuse at face value. Something about Uncle Warren could diminish Ruth's energy to a kind of jitteriness so that she'd fumble with things like silverware when clearing the table, things she didn't otherwise think twice about.

Surveying the good silver, Blake said, "She's never fussed quite this much over him, has she?"

Vickie examined one of the spoons, a bucolic scene in relief of deer drinking along a stream. The spoons were from Ruth's great-great-grandmother's wedding silver. "She doesn't have Mom to fuss over, I guess."

"She'd laugh so, if she could see us all now."

"Mom?"

"At how serious we've become. Serious in our own ridiculous ways." Blake sent the cradle rocking on the table. "Remember those tremendous sand castles we'd build? She'd laugh and laugh, saying, 'Can you imagine if it was a real castle?' "

Blake continued to rock the cradle pensively, and Vickie remembered him putting the finishing touches on the turrets long after Vickie and Meryl had tired of the castle. The tide would come in and wash it away, and Lydia liked to be the first to collapse what was left of the turrets by stamping on them. Blake would sit back in the sand looking devastated, and Vickie would be reminded of how her parents were so different.

But it was exactly their differences that had brought them together in the first place when they met at a club dance. Blake had come as a guest since he was from Sladebrook, and Lydia asked him to dance, spotting him standing alone "looking like he was having his teeth extracted."

"She led me in the tango," Blake liked to add whenever Lydia would tell this story, smiling thoughtfully as he rolled a cigarette between his fingers.

"Oh, I didn't *lead* you . . . ," Lydia would say, taking his cigarette and pretending to smoke. Having quit smoking, she blew invisible smoke rings.

In one way or another, Lydia had always been

pulling Vickie's father out onto the dance floor, allowing him to surprise himself. In front of other people, he was uncomfortable with any gesture more demonstrative than a caress of her neck, and sometimes Lydia liked to embarrass him by climbing into his lap. Blake, gently trying to nudge her off, would then laugh as Ruth left the room mumbling, "Goodness, can't you save that for a second honeymoon?"

Vickie was less sure what it was about her father that her mother had so loved. Maybe it was partly that, her satisfaction in being able to draw him out of himself. And maybe it was something else, how he could occasionally draw her in. He liked to beachcomb and on one of their family walks, Vickie remembered him giving her a piece of driftwood he thought was in the shape of a lizard. For a moment she examined it with some interest, as occasionally she would his lamps at the store, especially the kerosene student ones with decorative glass shades and chimneys.

But as if she couldn't see the lizard after all, she tossed aside the driftwood, and Vickie had felt suddenly cold as she used to when she'd hear them fighting on those nights after Blake first quit the firm.

"You're supposed to be taking care of me. Is this how you think you're taking care of me?" Her mother would yell as Vickie and Meryl huddled together on the landing of the stairs.

"You don't need to be taken care of, Lydia," her

father said. "Not in the way you mean, anyway."

"I don't want you hanging around the house! That's not what you're supposed to be doing, hanging around the house!"

"And what am I supposed to do? According to who?"

Lydia wouldn't answer, storming up the stairs, and Vickie and Meryl would quickly run back to their rooms.

There were no midnight baths then, and her mother would go sleep in their great-grandmother's old room. Vickie and Meryl would sneak into each other's bed, trying to warm their feet together.

"Dad? Do you think about seeing other people?"

Blake stilled the cradle, cupping his hand over it. "I couldn't."

"You think she'd be angry?"

"I don't know. I only know I can still hear her, like with the castles. Like now. Laughing."

It hurt Vickie to see how in love he still was with her mother. She'd known how in love he'd been by the small things he used to do for her, like planting a fir tree. He didn't care to have much to do with gardening, but Lydia was so against the cutting down of trees that every year he'd plant one in the backyard to transplant into a pot at Christmas.

"Maybe you'll stop hearing her," Vickie said.

"Have you?" he asked irritably.

Vickie looked out the window. Four years ago, Lydia had ripped up the backyard to plant wildflowers. Vickie was home visiting, and she remembered watching her mother sprinkle seeds from a single can. "There'll even be bluebells," Lydia said, reading off the contents.

Since then, there had been no bluebells whatsoever, only a few scraggly black-eyed Susans and daisies choked by knee-high weeds. Blake had always hated the weeds; every spring he threatened to resod the lawn. But yesterday, Vickie saw him out there supporting the head of a new black-eyed Susan between two fingers.

Three dogs were suddenly tearing through the weeds, and in a moment Gail appeared. She emerged from the trees gradually as if materializing out of the leafy darkness. There was first the glint of her auburn hair, then her face as pale as a gray sky reflected in Ruth's old, cracked cement birdbath.

CHAPTER 10

CAN'T YOU at least put them on leashes?" Ruth complained. She'd brought out a bowl of soapy water and was sponging the porch table. "Piper doesn't appreciate them, I assure you."

"Give them a minute; they'll calm down," Gail said, flinging back her braid. "And Piper, I think, can take care of himself—from what you've told me lately, he rules the neighborhood or at least the cat doors."

"It's all the girls," Blake said, tossing a stick to

the Irish setter. "She's remarkable—can catch in midair."

The dog ignored the stick, squatting by the old well.

"Mindy's temperamental lately," Gail said.

"Well, we all have our moments," Blake said, heading around to the side of the house. "Might as well take a look at that shed."

Vickie stroked the Lab. Labradors had been her favorite to work with when she assisted as a trainer, since most of the dogs were spoiled poodles or Pekingeses.

"That's Clara," Gail said. "And very clever. Knows just how to unlatch that gate. She can disappear for hours at a time."

"She must be something besides Lab," Vickie said, noticing the white patch on her chest.

"I know, she's really a mutt, I suppose, though I hate that word."

The white reached up the dog's throat into an almost perfect diamond. "She's beautiful."

"She is, isn't she?" Gail said, sounding very pleased.

"Can you imagine, Gail with dogs?" Ruth said.

"So, I hear you quit your job, Vickie," Gail said.

"You *quit* your job?" Ruth exclaimed.

"I vamoosed, I decamped, I flew the coop."

"And when did you think you were going to make this announcement?"

"I already knew your reaction."

Ruth wrung out her rag only to dip it back into the water.

"Well, good for you, dear," Gail said. "There's no point in being unhappy."

"The only job your grandfather ever had was at the clock factory," Ruth said. "There weren't so many choices back then. You kids are plagued with too many choices."

"He *owned* the factory," Vickie said.

"How can you have too many choices, anyway?" Gail said. "I say, make as many choices as you can. Think of all the things I could have done if I hadn't married so young."

"Oh, you always let her off too easy," Ruth said, leaning on the table to scrub a stubborn spot of bird dropping.

Gail winked at Vickie.

Vickie was grateful to Gail for always having been so yielding, for showing her a kind of understanding she'd missed from her own mother. When she was thirteen, Gail was the one to offer her a job weeding to pay back the money she stole from her mother's purse for a round-trip bus ticket to Boston, that time she'd cut school so she could spend the day in a place where no one recognized her.

Every day for a week after school, Vickie knelt in Gail's driveway, pulling up spindly dandelions from the gravel, and Gail would bring her glasses of lemonade. One day she lingered there, and while rinsing out the garbage cans with the hose, she asked, "So what did you do in Boston?"

Until then, Gail hadn't spoken to her, as if that, too, were part of her punishment. Vickie didn't know whether she was really expected to answer.

"Where'd you go?" Gail persisted.

"I rode the T."

"Well . . . to where?"

Vickie examined her knuckles, sore from grating against the gravel. The fact was, she hadn't known where to go. "Back and forth over the Charles."

Gail turned over the can emptying the water. "So you were the Invisible Man?"

"The Invisible Man?"

"Well, that's what I like about cities, feeling like you can go anywhere and do anything you want without anyone ever really knowing."

On the T, the people sitting across from Vickie had stared blindly as if they couldn't see her at all. "And people wondered why the doors opened and closed all by themselves," she said, unable to keep from smiling.

Gail laughed, kneeling beside Vickie. She began pulling up weeds, and Vickie looked at her.

"Well, don't tell your mother, okay?"

Vickie had a feeling of camaraderie then that she'd only ever had with this one girl from school;

they'd cut gym class together to escape having to do floor-mat routines. Both of them were particularly clumsy at vaulting and backflips, her friend too stout, while Vickie was too tall. This girl wasn't one to cut classes, and she'd try hard to fit in with the other girls, edging her way into their lunch tables even though they'd complain she smelled of old lady's talcum powder. But she actually tried smoking one of Vickie's cigarettes, and Vickie had felt as pleased as having Gail help her weed.

"I think about that now, of doing something I've never done before, just getting up and going somewhere," Gail said.

"You should then," Vickie said.

"Well, now I can't; not with these dogs."

"Those dogs," Ruth said, frowning.

"I'm afraid we have rats," Blake said, coming back around from the shed.

"Rats?" exclaimed Ruth. "We don't have rats."

"Anyone can have rats," Gail said. "We've had them at one time or another in our cellar."

"The shed floor is all dug up—a mound of dirt," Blake said. "Do we have any bacon?"

"What do you need bacon for?" Ruth asked. "Yes, we have bacon."

"To set traps," he answered, brushing past her to go inside.

"Gail, those dogs are trampling my garden," Ruth complained.

Gail stretched out on a lounge chair. "They're *exploring*."

It was hard to imagine Gail with dogs, and Vickie couldn't help asking, "So what made you decide to get them all?"

"Oh, I don't know really. I just know the difference they make."

The Lab, Clara, lay sprawled on the porch and Vickie stroked her ears. They were smooth as silk. "Since Mom?"

"She would have approved, wouldn't she?" Gail said. "If only because she'd be pleased at how they've already scratched up all my wood floors—she'd wanted to scratch them up herself, if just to spite Jeffrey, with those heels of hers."

"We found them all, Mom's shoes," Vickie said.

"All those shoes . . . ," Ruth said ruminatively.

"Oh Lydia. I told her she should show up at the club in my favorite, those orange pumps, and shock the Guccis off everyone else."

"They were so unlike her," Ruth said, shaking her head.

"That's why she bought them. Because they *were* unlike her," Gail said.

Ruth brushed at a spot on the old robe as if it weren't already stained. "Is that so."

From the time of that dinner party when Jeffrey threw his glass at the wall, Ruth had been distrustful of Gail. On those mornings Gail came by for breakfast, if Ruth didn't have a meeting or club luncheon, she would stay upstairs. For the most part, she'd been able to avoid Gail over the years, but after the accident, they finally had to confront each other when Gail told her that Lydia's wish had been for her ashes to be scattered in the ocean.

"The *ocean?*" Ruth said.

"We were walking along the beach—"

"The beach? You were walking along the beach? She'll be buried in the family plot. She wanted to be buried with her family. Of course she wanted that, to be buried in the plot."

"You mean, you *assume* she wanted that," Gail said.

Ruth began to shake so violently then, Vickie was afraid she might be having a seizure. *"I knew my daughter!"*

Gail hadn't said anything more, retreating into the silence they all retreated into those first days when Ruth could burst into a rage over a burned pot holder.

Lydia's ashes were buried in the plot, and Vickie, too, found it hard to believe her mother would have wanted it any other way. Lydia had been the one who most faithfully remembered to buy wreaths every Christmas and white lilies at Easter to place on the headstones.

But Vickie knew what close friends her mother and Gail had been, despite their friendship seeming to have been based more on a mutual need than on anything they had in common. After Gail's husband first moved out and her son left for Texas, Lydia sometimes spent the night over at her house until Gail grew more used to being alone. And years earlier, when Blake first quit the firm, Lydia was over at Gail's so often Vickie could count on finding her there after school. She began to wonder now whether Gail perhaps had known her mother better than anyone.

Blake came back outside with the bacon, as well as a hanger and an old plastic birdseed pail. They watched as he trimmed the hanger to slip through two holes in the pail's lip. He wound the bacon around the hanger.

"Is this another one of your inventions?" Ruth asked.

"No, it's not another one of my inventions. It's Tony's. Tony Moore."

"He came and set up the same thing in our cellar," Gail said. "You fill the pails with water, and when the rats try to get the bacon, they fall in and drown."

"How dreadful," Ruth said.

"I saw him trap a couple of stray cats once," Blake said. "He made a pretty decent living at just that, trapping animals. I think he's retired now, down to Florida."

"Florida—what is it about Florida? Everyone leaves town and then see what happens," Ruth said, nodding in the direction of the Arnolds'.

Gail laughed. "Who knows, maybe they really are Mafia. What with that designer clothes outlet they want to build that's bound to attract more tourists, soon maybe we really won't know who our neighbors are."

"See?" Ruth adjusted her dish towel as if it were one of her hats that her own mother had worn, with bluebirds perched around their rims. "They'll no doubt be putting in one of those large saucers next."

"I can't imagine the Mafia shopping at an outlet when they can afford to shop at the real thing," Blake said.

"Saucers? What saucers?" Gail asked.

"She means a satellite dish," Blake said. "As if that would be so extraordinary."

"*I* haven't seen those saucers in anyone's backyard," Ruth said.

"That's because you don't get out anymore," Blake said. "All you do is sit in that car."

As if she'd run out of better things to do, Ruth picked out dried pieces of root from one of the empty flower boxes lining the railing. The petunias she'd bought to fill them had been sitting in the wheelbarrow since Vickie arrived, Ruth never having been as fond of gardening as Lydia.

"Gramma, why don't you get involved in something again?" Vickie asked.

"Your granddaughter's right," Gail said. "I thought you would have been particularly concerned about that—the outlet. They talk about busing day trips in from Boston."

"I don't need your counseling, thank you. Just like I don't need this party."

Taking the pail, Blake quickly disappeared around to the shed.

"Who ever *needs* a party? You just like to make a fuss," Gail said.

Ruth gazed out at the dogs as they rustled their way through her lilac bushes.

"It might be good for you, Ruth," Gail said more gently.

"At least it's an excuse to fox-trot," Vickie said.

Ruth started to smile but then said, "Gail, please rein in those animals. I'd appreciate not having to step in their business later."

"Oh, fuss, fuss, fuss."

Gail slapped her thigh and whistled piercingly, and Vickie thought how unlike her to make such a display. It was more like Gail to sit as quietly as she used to at their barbecues as if listening for a particular sound, some faint dripping of water from the maple leaves.

Clara leaped at Vickie to lick her face. "She's a real sweetie, isn't she?"

"And terribly sensitive," Gail said. "She can sulk for hours under the table."

"Goodness, the way you talk," Ruth said.

"If I'm so off my rocker, what about you? Blake told me how you've hidden the keys to that car. You probably don't even remember where."

Ruth tentatively touched her lip as if indeed she had forgotten. Then she said, "My point is, they're not *human*, Gail."

The sun shifted through the maple, and Vickie remembered how Gail had seemed to waver precariously, to break up and dissolve into the shadows, that night when she'd streaked up the hill in only her nightgown. "Why don't you leave her alone about the dogs?"

"And why, Victoria, have you always shown her more respect than you could show your own mother?"

"*Ruth . . . ,*" Gail snapped.

Vickie felt herself growing pale.

Her grandmother looked around as if she'd lost something, picking up the empty flower box to set it down again. "I should hose down that car. The pollen from that cherry blossom is ruining it." She went around to the front of the house.

A feeling of utter helplessness welled up inside Vickie as it could when she least expected it, when she was cooking rice and staring into the water waiting for it to boil. As if it were all still so new, and her mother's wheelbarrow was where she'd left it that day when she'd driven up for the fertilizer. It remained there for weeks afterward, half hidden by the forsythia bushes.

"Your grandmother just has to have the last word on everything, you know that," Gail said.

Vickie stroked Clara's ears, comforted by their silky feel.

"Oh, you and your mother were just too alike, Vickie," Gail said, taking the spaniel into her lap.

"*Alike?*" Vickie laughed, trying to fight back tears. "We couldn't agree on anything."

"That's just it—when you two disagreed, it was like dodging your reflection in the mirror." Gail inspected the spaniel's eyelids in that absent way Vickie had seen her sister examine Daryll when he'd fallen asleep in her arms. "Half the reason, you know, your mother was so upset over Kyle was because she liked him."

"Kyle? All she did was complain about him."

"She complained too much—she'd talk about

him all the time. She just no more knew what to expect from him than she did from you, and that drove her crazy."

"Well, if she liked Kyle so much, why'd she give me such a hard time?" Vickie asked.

"What would Ruth have thought?"

"*Gramma* likes Kyle; she's even invited him to the party."

"But would she ever admit to it?"

Vickie reluctantly let Clara bound off into the weeds.

"There just isn't any talking to your grand-mother sometimes," Gail said. "Like when you had some recital, and it was your turn to do the dishes. Your mother wanted to do them for you, but Ruth convinced her that was no way to learn responsi-bility. As if your grandmother's so terribly respon-sible herself."

Vickie remembered that. She'd missed the be-ginning of the recital. And she remembered how angry she'd been, not with Ruth, but with her mother.

Vickie had never thought of her mother and her-self as being the least bit alike, except for when Vickie was little, and there were those brief moments when they came together, such as when Lydia would find her down in the basement making "machines" out of boxes and filling jelly jars with water and food coloring; mostly Lydia worried about all the time

Vickie spent alone down there, but Vickie remembered how pleased she had looked holding up a jar of water she'd mixed herself into her favorite orange, the orange of an "October setting sun."

And there were those occasional times when her mother actually seemed to have arrived at some kind of acceptance of her. Once when Vickie was home from school after having her wisdom teeth pulled, she found herself able to think out loud with her mother, saying, "There was a tooth found once over a million years old." Feeling better, Vickie was helping shell shrimp for a potluck supper at the church, and they had fallen into a comfortable silence punctuated by the dropping of shells into the steel bowl.

"Really . . . ," Lydia said, picking out a piece of shell from her nail.

"From beneath a pile of dik-dik droppings." Vickie had been reading a paleontology book she'd picked up at the library's annual sale.

"A dik-dik?"

"It's a kind of antelope native to East Africa."

Smiling, Lydia patted Vickie's cheeks to feel whether the swelling had gone down. She'd changed the soaked bloody gauze wedged into Vickie's gums and made her teardrop noodles to slip down easily. "You're never dull, are you?"

Vickie had wanted to tell her more, about the kerais, the metal bowls of dirt the paleontologists would have to pick through by hand. But her mother was already getting up to empty the shrimp shells into the garbage, saying that the only kind of books she cared about reading at Vickie's age were love stories like *Gone with the Wind*. Stories that didn't interest Vickie in the least.

CHAPTER 11

UNCLE WARREN was so tall, he had to duck through the front door as if squeezing himself into a dollhouse, and he would have seemed gangly if he didn't have such a way of dwarfing everything around him. His features were as dramatic as Vickie knew her grandfather's had been from the pictures in the buffet. He had the same high forehead, long thin nose, and ears that stuck out slightly. Only his small beady eyes were Ruth's.

"Whose old T-bird?" he asked, setting down a

couple of suitcases large enough to hold clothes for
a month rather than a few days. He and his family
had driven up from Pennsylvania.

He stooped to kiss his mother. Ruth had changed
into one of her gossamer dresses she otherwise re-
served for club luncheons, and a yellowed lace handkerchief was folded into her breast pocket.

"Yours, Vickie?" he asked.

"Why would it be mine?"

"Weren't you always wanting an old car? There
was that Christmas when you were asking your parents for a loan to buy some beat-up old Ford that
needed 'only,' I think, 'a new transmission.' " He
laughed.

"I was a kid in school."

Shawna came in, and Vickie was always astonished at how little she could remember of what her
cousin looked like. In contrast to Uncle Warren, she
seemed entirely featureless, her face as plain as a
dinner plate. As a kid, she had been a tremendous
dawdler, lagging behind with some matted stuffed
animal dangling limply from one hand, and Vickie
and Meryl had largely ignored her.

Her son, Gordon, squirmed in her arms, twisting
her fine silver choker.

"Oh, what a little man he's become," Ruth said.

"More like a little terror," Shawna said, letting
him down. "We had to keep the windows shut

the entire way—he kept grabbing raisins, tissues, anything, to toss out."

Shawna's husband, Phillip, lugged in the last of the bags—a large fishnet sack bulging with plastic fruit, balls, and stuffed dinosaurs.

"Where's Anna?" Ruth asked.

"At the last minute she had to stay home," Uncle Warren said, scratching behind one ear so that it stuck out farther. "We're having the bedrooms painted."

"The bedrooms painted?"

"She didn't want to leave the house unoccupied."

"You made good time," Blake said, coming into the hall, brushing sawdust off his flannel shirt.

"Anna didn't come," Ruth said.

"Is she sick?"

"She's having the bedrooms painted," Ruth said, sounding more and more perplexed.

"So whose old car *is* that?" Uncle Warren asked, moving past them into the living room.

His eyes scanned the walls, and Vickie knew he was looking for new spots of buckling wallpaper. "Is that what you're fixing now these days, Blake, old cars?" Uncle Warren asked, rocking back and forth feeling for loose floorboards.

"Actually, Warren, it's your mother's car."

"Mother's?" Uncle Warren stopped rocking. "Mother, you don't drive anymore. . . ."

Ruth pressed her handkerchief flat, and everyone grew quiet. There had been this same cumbersome silence when last year Lydia made the mistake of consulting him about converting the porch into a greenhouse. "A *greenhouse?*" Uncle Warren had said. "You want to build a greenhouse when the rest of the house is falling apart?"

Gordon swiped the mussel shells off the end table.

Ruth covered her ears as if they had crashed to the floor rather than scattering soundlessly across the rug. "Well, he has become a terror, hasn't he?" She forced a laugh.

Phillip began picking up the shells, and he looked like a young boy kneeling there. He'd been trying to grow a beard since Vickie last saw him at Christmas, and now he had what amounted to little more than a fuzzy outline of his chin. "The fact is, he's too bright for his own good," Phillip said. "He'll see some commercial on TV, and two weeks later he'll be singing the D'Agastino's jingle. Word for word."

"I can't believe you bought a car, Mother," Uncle Warren said. "So what kind of deal did you get on it?" He looked out at the Thunderbird. "They couldn't have asked for very much—the bottom's rusted through; I can see it from here."

"What does it matter what kind of deal? It was something she wanted," Vickie said, unable to believe she was actually trying to make sense out of the fact that her grandmother had bought a car she couldn't drive.

"Never mind, dear," Ruth said, kneading the handkerchief now so that it began to wilt. "Why don't you all go out on the porch and I'll bring out the melon."

"We've had a hundred thousand dollars' worth of copper wire ripped out from streetlights." Phillip worked for the Pennsylvania Department of Transportation and was recounting for them the latest rash of highway robberies. He was so fair his face was a map of tiny blood vessels, and he'd borrowed one of Ruth's large-brimmed sun hats.

"Fire hydrants, too. They take apart fire hydrants," Shawna added, trying to keep Gordon from smearing melon down his Batman shirt.

"It's become a national problem. All the scrap dealers are on the lookout now, but it's hard to know what is and isn't actually stolen." Phillip shook his head gravely. "They're even taking out chain-link fences and the aluminum guardrails."

"Can you get that much for aluminum?" Blake asked.

"Enough for a hit of crack. That's at the root of it, the cocaine epidemic."

"That's not the *real* root of it," Shawna said. "The real root is the state of the economy. The poor are getting poorer, and as long as that keeps happening, it's going to be one long downward spiral into addiction."

Uncle Warren laughed. "My daughter, the eternal optimist."

"Dad doesn't see that even people in his own income bracket are losing their jobs, facing foreclosures on their homes," Shawna said. "I know someone who was an investment banker and now works for a moving company. And he's renting an apartment in the same building where he'd once owned a condominium."

"With the real-estate market so depreciated, I would think architects would be the first to feel it," Vickie said.

Uncle Warren took out his pocket watch. The watch had belonged to Vickie's grandfather, and Vickie didn't remember when Uncle Warren wasn't wearing it attached to that gold chain.

"We've had to lay off fourteen people in the last three months," he said, turning the watch over in his hand as if expecting it to be scratched or damaged. He slipped it back into his pocket. "I didn't say we weren't feeling it. I just think things will turn around."

"Now who's the eternal optimist?" Shawna said.

"Oh, your generation is so spoiled, anyway," Ruth said, as she had when Vickie had forfeited the money her grandmother had put toward her tuition by dropping out of college. "Look at Vickie, going and giving up a perfectly good job."

"I'm not paying off a mortgage," Vickie said.

"You quit your job?" Uncle Warren said. "Your mother always said you were the eye of a hurricane, never knowing when it was going to hit."

Vickie knew her mother had regularly consulted Uncle Warren about "handling" her. He'd talked Lydia out of a loan for Vickie to buy that Ford, as he'd talked her out of building the greenhouse.

Gordon let out a piercing scream, swatting Shawna for not letting him yank the heads off the potted geraniums.

"I'll take him," Phillip said getting up, holding onto the sun hat as if there were a strong breeze. He dug out a Nerf ball from the fishnet bag.

Handing Gordon to him, Shawna went limp as if she'd been carrying heavy boxes. "He's seeing a therapist."

"Phillip?" Ruth asked.

"Gordon."

"A therapist? He's only three," Ruth said.

"He won't leave the house. He won't let me out of his sight." Shawna picked up a plastic pineapple and dangled it by its stem the way she used to dangle her stuffed animals. "What's coming out is, somehow he's never forgotten those first seven months I worked full time."

Shawna was a physical therapist, and when

Gordon was learning to walk, Vickie remembered her turning two chairs onto their sides for railings and coaxing him along like someone in leg braces.

"You mean he's been scarred for life?" Vickie laughed, not realizing how sarcastic she sounded until Ruth glared at her. "I mean, there are plenty of working mothers whose kids turn out all right."

"Yes, it doesn't do a whole lot for the women's movement, does it?" Shawna said. "All I know is, now I'm working only part-time, and he's great with the baby-sitter. But when it's just the two of us, all he wants is to play down in the basement with the lights off, pretending I'm a water witch. I have to crawl on all fours looking for fluorescent yellow jacks balls."

Gail's dogs interrupted Phillip and Gordon's game of Nerf, and in a few moments Gail emerged from the woods.

"Since when do you have dogs?" Uncle Warren asked her as she came up to the porch.

"Since they captured my heart. Although I'm cross right now with Clara—she ran away again this morning and was gone almost three hours."

"Clara?"

"This one," Vickie said, patting her diamond of white.

Gail set a colander of strawberries on the railing. "First pick of the season, all washed and ready to eat."

"What a nice treat," Shawna said, taking the colander and passing it around. Vickie knew she didn't care much for Gail, unable to understand why her hair had to be quite so long.

"Do you know she makes their dinners from scratch?" Ruth said. "Veal stew. She actually makes them veal stew."

Tired of her grandmother's relentless harping on the dogs, Vickie changed the subject. "Shawna was just telling us that Gordon's seeing a therapist."

Uncle Warren laughed. "So now when he knocks things off tables, they ask him what he's 'feeling.' "

"Dad thinks it's all a joke," Shawna said.

"I just don't know what happened to good old-fashioned discipline. Like when Father used to take the hairbrush to us—it hardly hurt, in fact, didn't leave a mark. Only a lasting impression."

"Where's Anna, inside?" Gail asked.

"Anna's having the bedrooms painted," Ruth said. "She didn't want to leave the house alone."

"Oh, well . . . ," Gail said vaguely. "Once I left the house while the tiles were being replaced in the bathroom, and I never again saw the cracked ceramic toothbrush holder I'd saved in the cabinet there. Although why anyone would want—"

"She's never missed a single holiday," Ruth said.

"It's not exactly a holiday, Mother," Uncle Warren said.

Ruth pressed her handkerchief flat.

"Why don't you just tell them, Dad," Shawna said.

Uncle Warren slipped his hand into his pocket feeling for the watch. "Anna and I are separating."

As if she'd been poked in the back, Ruth stiffened. *"Separating?"*

"Ever since she started taking scuba lessons."

"This is Aunt Anna's idea?" Vickie said, finding it hard to imagine Aunt Anna mustering such courage. She knew her best as staying literally a step behind Uncle Warren, resting her hand on his back as if gently nudging open a door.

"She seems to need some time to herself," Uncle Warren said. "Although I don't understand why she can't take scuba lessons without disrupting our lives."

"You know it's more than that, Dad," Shawna said quietly.

"Anna's afraid of water," Blake said. "We could never even get her into the bay, and it's only waist high."

"It's not water she's afraid of," Shawna explained. "She swims at the pool all the time. She's just always been afraid of the ocean. That's why she's taking lessons, to get over that fear."

"That's great," Vickie said.

"What's so great about it?" Ruth said, pacing the

porch. "A divorce. I can't believe you're actually getting a divorce."

"Oh, don't be so dramatic, Mother. We're still under the same roof," Uncle Warren said.

"A *divorce*. We've never had a divorce in the family."

"For God's sake, Mother, why do you pretend you're so concerned with appearances?"

"How can you let this happen?"

"How can *I* let this happen?"

"You just built that house together. You just put in that Jacuzzi. Doesn't that mean anything, that you just built a house together?"

"Don't talk to me about this, talk to Anna!" Uncle Warren left them to join in the game. How out of character he seemed running after a bright orange ball.

Ruth looked at Shawna. "What is she thinking? What is your mother thinking?"

"Gramma . . . ," Shawna began. "It's been a long time coming, okay?"

"Your parents have been married for thirty years."

Shawna looked stonily out at the yard.

"So look at me and Jeffrey," Gail said. "We were married twenty-five years and where did that get us—numbers don't matter."

"You and Jeffrey hardly count," Ruth said.

"Hardly count?"

"Your marriage was atypical."

Gail laughed. "Aren't most bad marriages?"

Ruth began neatly piling the melon rinds one within the other.

"We did love each other, believe it or not," Gail said. "He just didn't know how to love. Not in the right way."

"We're not talking about Jeffrey, we're talking about my son," Ruth said. "We're talking about a perfectly rational man who would never strike his wife."

Clara rested her head on Gail's chair. Gail made a move as if to pet the dog, but then fingered her palms, a habit she'd developed since the cuts there had healed from the fish tank's broken glass.

"It's none of your business, Gramma," Vickie said.

Red spots began to break out on Ruth's face. "And where'd you learn to talk to me like that?"

"It's *their* business. Uncle Warren's and Aunt Anna's."

"I'm your grandmother."

Vickie got up, needing to escape as urgently as if she had a full bladder. "Well, I guess I just don't show you any respect, either."

CHAPTER 12

FTER ALL THESE years, why now?"
Meryl asked, strapping Daryll into his
car seat and handing him his favorite
yellow measuring cup so that he wouldn't suck on
the strap. Vickie had come by to help with last-
minute shopping for the party and told her about
Uncle Warren.

"Aunt Anna probably got tired of pleasing him,"
Vickie said. "She just kept giving and giving, and
he never appreciated how much she gave."

"Oh, you've just always resented him."

"Why does he have to be so patronizing?"

"Uncle Warren's just being Uncle Warren."

"But even toward his own mother, giving her a hard time about that car."

"She went out and bought a car she can't *drive,* Vickie."

"Look," Alex said, dangling a dead grasshopper over the front seat.

"God, Alex," Meryl said.

"I found it out by the barn."

"Ever find any arrowheads?" Vickie asked.

"Arrowheads?"

"You're probably finding them all the time— they can look like any old rocks."

"I find rocks . . . ," Alex said.

"I found an arrowhead once and it ended up in the museum."

"The Marrow Museum," Meryl said. "That's now the children's library. What a silly museum that was, mostly old duck decoys."

"Was it from an Indian?" Alex asked.

Vickie nodded. "From one of the earliest settlers. Even before your great-great-great or however many great-grandmothers."

"Alex, put on your seat belt," Meryl said.

"I bet I've found tons of them," Alex said.

"Well, look for stones with blunted tips; dig a little deeper."

"Deeper?" Meryl said. "I think she digs deep enough. She doesn't need any more encouraging."

"There's no harm in her getting her hands dirty."

Trying to keep her distance from the car in front, Meryl couldn't help tailgating. She didn't need to hear from her sister about how she should be raising her own child.

"Anyway, so Gramma's a little eccentric," Vickie said. "That doesn't mean she can't take care of herself."

"She can't. At least not when it comes to paying attention to details, like balancing a checkbook."

"But Uncle Warren treated Mom that way, too."

"She couldn't balance a checkbook either, was forever bouncing checks."

"Maybe she'd been made to *think* she couldn't balance it. By her big brother."

"He's just being *Uncle Warren,* Vickie."

Vickie put her feet up on the dashboard, Meryl knew, to aggravate her—Meryl hated the ribbed footprints her sneakers would leave there, even though the dashboard was already marred with the black outlines of old cereal box stickers.

"Gordon's seeing a therapist," Vickie said.

"A therapist?"

"All because Shawna was working full-time those first few months. But they've always been neurotic about him anyway, especially after you told

Shawna some horror story last year about a kid choking on a marble, and she kept inspecting his mouth every half hour."

"Well, those first few months are crucial, when you're supposed to be bonding with your child."

Vickie just stared at her.

"What?" Meryl asked.

"Why do you always have to take such a panoramic view of things?"

"Panoramic?"

"Like with Uncle Warren," Vickie said. "You make so many excuses for him."

"He doesn't mean half the things he says, Vickie. Just like the rest of us don't mean half the things we say." The kids had grown so quiet, Meryl glanced in the rearview mirror. Daryll was balancing the cup on his head and Alex was drawing invisible pictures on the window. "It's just this kinetic energy this family has, like we're one big imploding star."

"See? You're so busy being fair, you never see anything close up."

"If I wasn't so fair, Victoria, you all would have been at each other's throats *long* ago." Meryl stepped on the gas to pass the car in front of her.

"Geez, Mel."

"The lane's clear."

"I know. You've just never done that before."

"Told ya," Alex whispered, leaning over the front seat toward Vickie.

"Told her *what?*"

"That you pass cars . . . ," Alex said dejectedly, and Meryl wished she hadn't snapped so. But she didn't appreciate Alex now confiding in Vickie not only about where she goes on her bike but about her own mother.

Alex didn't say anything more until they were turning into the parking lot. "The pond's gone."

"The pond?" Meryl asked.

"Me and Aunt Vickie went wading."

"You went wading in a parking lot? You could have stepped in glass."

"Well, we didn't, did we?" Vickie said.

Meryl took Daryll from the backseat and slammed the car door. "Wait until you have a kid."

Vickie laughed. "I can wait."

Alex climbed onto the yellow-spotted pony outside of the market. "Can I have a quarter? Please?"

"There isn't time, sweetie, we have a lot to do," Meryl said, sliding Daryll into the seat of a cart.

"I'll be right in," Vickie said, running back across the parking lot. Kyle was getting into his van.

They leaned against the van talking, the way they used to lean against the maple in Ruth's backyard. From the upstairs bathroom window Meryl had been able to see how Kyle would brace Vickie at the base of her spine and move his fingers down around her buttocks.

Imagining him touching Vickie like that again, Meryl wanted to disappear inside the market. She felt mired there, her hands gripping the cart so that her knuckles turned white.

It had been a couple of months since Meryl first ran into Kyle, at the wedding reception of an old friend from the club. He'd been hired as the photographer, and how displaced he'd looked wearing a T-shirt with bright red suspenders and probably his only good pair of pants, faded black corduroys. Yet he had seemed so at ease, not hesitating to pile a napkin with the last of the stuffed mushrooms.

Meryl herself had felt entirely uncomfortable, even though her friends there were as familiar to her as the games they used to play together in the club pool, maybe because it was the first wedding she remembered having to attend without Glenn, who was home with the flu.

She'd wondered whether she, too, was coming down with it, feeling warm and light-headed as a couple of her friends compared the prices they'd researched on installing laundry chutes. It was what her mother probably would have called an "inane" conversation, and as they went on to discuss microwave ovens, Meryl wondered what made them such good friends at all. Beyond the memories they shared of playing in the pool, they seemed to share little else. Suddenly overwhelmed by the confusion of patterns, the paisley peach curtains and floral tablecloths, she got up thinking she'd escape to the blank walls of the ladies' room. She found herself going over to Kyle who was reloading his camera.

She didn't remember what they talked about, probably not very much and certainly not about Vickie. But she had been surprised to find him more attractive than she remembered. She forgot her feeling of light-headedness, imagining what it must be like to view the all-too-familiar scene from his end of the lens.

Kyle glanced in Meryl's direction, and Meryl abruptly wheeled her cart around. "Let's go in now."

"Mommy, please, one quarter."

Meryl looked at her daughter and was startled by how sorry she suddenly felt. Alex had grown too big for the pony, her feet pulled up in the stirrups so that her knees stuck out bonily. She gripped the pony's ears.

"Here," Meryl said, fumbling in her purse. She handed Alex a quarter.

"There's time?"

"There's time . . . ," Meryl said, all the energy sapped out of her so that she wanted to sit down. She leaned heavily on the cart and let Daryll twist the buttons on her blouse.

"You could have gone inside," Vickie said breathlessly, after running back across the lot.

"She wanted a ride," Meryl said, not looking at her sister. She watched the pony lurch awkwardly up and down as if something were caught in its mechanism.

"Ruth's invited him to your party, you know."

"Ruth? She doesn't even like Kyle. . . ."

"I think she's more open-minded than that."

"She couldn't stand him, Vickie."

"*You* couldn't stand him."

"That's enough, Alex," Meryl said.

"The ride's not over."

"I'll wait with her, Mel," Vickie said.

"Fine."

Meryl went inside, but not without glancing out through the discount signs taped on the window. Vickie was giving Alex another quarter.

CHAPTER 13

IT WASN'T THAT Meryl "couldn't stand" Kyle. It was just that back when Vickie first began seeing Kyle, she hadn't been able to figure out what her sister could see in someone who lived above an old gas station when he perfectly well could afford something more civilized. And although Meryl couldn't help worrying as their mother had about Vickie seeing someone twice her age, she hadn't meant to tell their mother about seeing Kyle pick Vickie up after school. Something Vickie had never been able to believe.

It was on a Sunday morning after Vickie had left for another "rehearsal" when her mother asked Meryl, "Why wouldn't she want us there?" Vickie had just tried to discourage their parents from attending the opening of her play.

"Well, she *is* only in the chorus," Meryl said, parroting Vickie's own excuse.

"Still . . ." Lydia propped the puzzle cover against the couch to see the picture. She and Meryl were sitting on the floor and had spread the pieces out across the coffee table. "I guess it just doesn't matter that much to her, whether we're there or not."

"Of course it matters . . . ," Meryl began.

Her mother nudged the puzzle pieces around the table without trying to connect them.

"She's not in the play."

Lydia looked at her.

"She's not in it," Meryl shrugged.

"What do you mean? What do you mean she's not in it?"

Meryl didn't answer, and Lydia lifted Meryl's chin so she would have to look at her. "Kyle?"

Meryl nodded. "Please, Mom—"

"It's all right, you should tell me. My God, how else am I to know what's going on with my own daughter?"

Eventually Meryl would perhaps have told her

anyway, after carefully weighing the consequences. But at that moment, she hadn't been able to bear how hurt her mother seemed, pushing around the puzzle pieces like so many fragments of something broken, something she couldn't put back together.

By the time Glenn came inside for dinner that night, Daryll was already asleep and Meryl had told Alex to get ready for bed. He'd had to bury two more carcasses he'd found when he was locking the chickens into the coop.

"Goddamn dog," he said, finally sitting down to eat. "The answer is, I'm going to have to set up some kind of pen."

"They'd be better in a pen, anyway," Meryl said.

Glenn didn't say anything, and she guessed his thoughts were already gearing toward its construction.

"Aunt Anna's leaving Uncle Warren."

"Oh, yeah? And why shouldn't she?"

Meryl should have figured Glenn wouldn't be surprised; he could no more tolerate Uncle Warren than Vickie could.

"He'll probably get through the wire, too."

"They're just chickens, Glenn."

"And it was Ruth who talked you into talking me into raising them."

There wasn't much Meryl could say to that, since

her mother was actually the one to convince them. Ruth had passed on to Lydia the article about unsanitary poultry inspection.

"They're an investment," Glenn said.

"So is that house."

Glenn picked a spot of candle wax off the tablecloth. He didn't usually notice things like that, and Meryl felt as sorry as she'd felt watching Alex riding the too-small pony.

"How'd it go, anyway?" Meryl asked.

"How'd what go?"

"Over at the house today."

"It went fine."

"You like how the tile looks?"

He nodded. "It will blend all right."

She'd tried to persuade him toward a more neutral color than lavender for the bathroom. "Well, it might actually make the sale for some buyer who'd have trouble coming up with his own color schemes," she said.

Glenn looked at her for a long moment, and she began picking off the rest of the candle wax herself. "Did you get that door up?"

The door was one of his favorite finds, pure oak with an octagonal stained-glass window.

"I put that up some time ago."

"Well, I'll have to drive by and see how it looks."

"You don't have to drive by," he said, smiling.

"You'd rather I didn't?"

"I just don't remember you being so interested in what exactly goes on over there—beyond the fact that I'm getting things done."

"I know," she said, feeling defeated. "It's just so long now since we've had any real cash flow through here. That keeps me a little on edge. I can't help it."

"Don't you think it keeps me on edge, too? I'm doing the best I can, Mel."

"I know," she said, placing her hand on his. "That's all I'm saying—I *do* know."

They linked fingers. "Well, what's the occasion?"

"Occasion for what?"

"This," he said, squeezing her hand.

"Am I that terrible?"

"Not terrible. A little unpredictable these days, maybe." He leaned over to kiss her. "But not terrible."

"Look, Daddy," Alex said, shuffling over to them in her big fuzzy slippers with the rabbit ears. She opened her pink box on Glenn's lap to show him the grasshopper.

Mel laughed. "How appetizing."

"Well, look at that, Pumpkin," Glenn said, holding it up to the light before giving it back to Alex.

"I'm looking for arrowheads now, too."

"Arrowheads?"

"Vickie's idea," Meryl said.

"You know where I bet you'd find arrowheads?"

Glenn said. "In that field over at the old Engels farm. It once was an Indian site."

"And it's also quite far away," Meryl said.

"She doesn't have to bike; I'd take her."

Meryl got up to clear the table. "You know she'll try to go on her own."

"No, I *won't*," Alex said, stamping on the grasshopper. She looked at Meryl so hatefully, Meryl snapped, "Get to bed, Alex, it's late."

Alex peeled away the grasshopper from the bottom of her slipper.

"Here," Glenn said, holding out his hand, and she placed it in his palm. "Still has its shape," he said, delicately tucking the grasshopper into a compartment of the makeup box. "Now go pick out a jungle book and I'll be in in a minute."

From the sound of Alex's long skating steps back to her room, Meryl knew that once again her father had made everything okay.

Meryl piled the plates into the sink, deciding she'd leave them for Glenn. "Between you and Vickie, I carry no weight."

"You worry so."

"And you let her do whatever it is she wants."

He didn't say anything.

"Something could happen to her, Glenn, the way she's all over the place."

"She's a kid on her bike, Mel."

"She's a kid on her bike collecting dead things."

"She's creating her own experiences; you have to admire that," Glenn said. "You just don't want to see her grow up."

"So it's me?"

"A lot of it is, I think."

"And *you're* not the one who has to keep track of her."

Glenn got up to clear his own plate.

"I better get over there," Meryl said, thinking he'd probably forgotten that she wanted to drive over to the hall and begin setting up. Something she wasn't actually going to do until tomorrow morning.

Glenn's voice was suddenly so deep and quiet, she hardly recognized it. "This isn't us, you know."

"We're discussing our daughter."

Glenn began rinsing the dishes.

"I won't be long," Meryl said.

He didn't turn around from the sink.

Meryl went out but sat in their driveway with the motor running. There was an almost full moon and she could see the branches of the magnolia tree reflected in one of the mirrors. They wavered so in a breeze, she felt she could dip her hand in and swirl around the reflection.

She drove off knowing how relieved she would feel once she pulled into Kyle's driveway and found herself not caring again. What she didn't know was that Kyle had forgotten to leave on the porch light for her. And his van was gone.

CHAPTER 14

VICKIE HAD DROPPED BY unexpectedly, and Kyle insisted they drive down to the beach because he'd done his laundry and his place was a "mess." He only had a rusted secondhand washing machine in the basement, and Vickie knew how his place looked when he had a clothesline draped across his living room, but she was just glad to escape Ruth and her uncle. At dinner, Ruth spoke to Uncle Warren only long enough to have the creamed peas passed down the table.

So many times before they'd sat in Kyle's van

like this, that pungent smell of wet wool mingled with the sharp scent of paint thinner. His dashboard was cluttered with the same things—a practically toothless comb, a couple of fish lures, and dried felt-tip pens. There were even the old plastic chess pieces they'd found together years ago while skating on Bell Lake. They were scattered across his dashboard as if they'd only recently been thrown there, and Vickie could have been sixteen again, when they would meet secretly, parking at the beach like this after Lydia had found out about them. Reminded of that, she felt the same rush of anger she'd felt earlier that day when she'd known Meryl was watching them from across the A&P parking lot. As if her sister still could tell on them to their mother.

"What were you thinking!" Vickie had yelled, bursting into Meryl's room after their mother had confronted her about Kyle.

Meryl was standing in front of her mirror trying to put up her hair that wasn't quite long enough.

"I didn't mean to tell her, Vickie."

"You didn't *mean* to?"

"She just worries about you so and we were just talking—"

"You two are always just talking."

Meryl wouldn't look at Vickie in the mirror.

"I didn't tell her about Glenn, did I?" Vickie said.

Meryl turned around. "What about Glenn?"

146

Vickie sat on her sister's bed, which was still piled high with old dolls, their faces marred by crayons Meryl had used to give them makeovers. "I saw your pills," Vickie said.

"You were going through my *things,* Victoria?"

"You didn't hide them very well, Meryl."

She'd discovered the birth control pills in the bottom of Meryl's shoe rack when she was borrowing back her thongs. How easily their mother, too, could have found them, but she had rarely searched Meryl's room as thoroughly as she did Vickie's.

Meryl seemed to have given up on her hair and was linking the hairpins across her bureau. Vickie knew it must be particularly distressing for her to think how betrayed their mother would feel. However disappointing Vickie proved herself to be, Meryl was the trustworthy one who was supposed to know better than to sleep with the man she loved before they were married. The only reason they weren't already married was because they were saving for a house. Both had graduated high school but were still living at home.

"You don't know what you're getting into, Victoria."

"Oh, skip the Victoria shit. And you didn't do this for me, Meryl. You did this for Mom—you just can't stand not to please her."

"And you can't stand once to make her happy!"

"See?" Vickie said, smiling with satisfaction.

Meryl threw one of her dolls at the door as Vickie left.

"The stars are falling," Kyle said. Jellyfish were being churned so violently in the surf, they sparkled.

"That's what we talked about the first time we kissed," Vickie said.

"Jellyfish?"

"The *stars*. We were at the beach like this and we could see the Milky Way. We started fighting over this one bright star. I thought it was the North Star and you said it was Jupiter."

"You know what the Milky Way really is?" They'd brought a six-pack, and Kyle held his empty bottle on its side. "It's just more stars, but everything's in the way you look at it. Here we are," he said, holding his finger perpendicular to the bottle. "And the bottle's the Milky Way. So we're actually looking *through* the stars."

"You don't remember?"

"I remember. And I remember thinking, What am I doing robbing the cradle?"

Vickie could tell he was smiling even though his face was in shadow. "Gail thinks Mom actually liked you."

"I think she probably did."

"You do? You never said that before. . . ."

He shrugged. "We were playing our respective

roles. I mean, liking me certainly wasn't something that was in the cards."

This was true, although Vickie wasn't sure why. Maybe only because liking Kyle never had been in the cards for her grandmother either, even now when she'd invited him.

"I want you to come to Gramma's party," she said.

"I'll think about it."

"Why is it such a big deal for you *not* to come?"

"It's really that important to you?"

"I'd like to see Meryl's face."

"That's not a good enough reason, Vickie."

They grew quiet for too long and Vickie said, "Let's walk."

When they were on the beach, she jumped onto his back. "Give me a ride."

"I'll give you a lift."

"No, I want a *ride,*" she insisted. This was an old joke between them, since Kyle had once told her that in Ireland, a guy offering a girl a ride didn't mean he wanted to give her a lift in his car but that he wanted to have sex.

"A lift! A lift! I'll give you a lift!" Kyle yelled, racing down the beach so that the sand spun away beneath her. He ran so fast, Vickie started to fall, and she pulled him down with her.

She kissed him. "Why is it that the only time I don't feel like I'm deposited here from another planet is when I'm with you?"

"My little romantic," he said, brushing back her hair.

"Don't make fun of me."

"I'm not making fun. You're always attributing things to me that have more to do with you, that's all. Like your photography—you know you're talented. From time to time, you just won't see that."

She moved her hand down between his legs.

"You're determined to seduce me, aren't you."

"You said you weren't serious about this woman you're seeing."

"I'm sleeping with her."

"I figured that," Vickie said, trying not to feel hurt. She unzipped his pants.

"Haven't you heard of AIDS?" he asked.

"Why are you trying so hard to ruin this?"

"I'm sorry. This just seems so easy for you."

"It always *was* easy with you. Besides. Aren't you still prepared for such emergencies?"

"They're in the van."

There were curtains on the windows so it was private in the back of the van. Kyle pushed aside the tools he kept there to spread out the old, red snowflake quilt they'd used ever since they first got friction burns from lying naked on the matted carpet.

He stripped off her shirt and jeans and knelt between her legs so he could stroke her stomach and breasts. Sliding off her underpants, he traced the curve of her hips and she felt beautiful. A feeling she sometimes found herself still getting used to, a feeling occasionally tinged with that same self-consciousness of their first "date," walking along Bell Lake when she became painfully aware that she was somewhat taller than he. When the only thing she could think of to talk about was the old boathouse.

"There's no boathouse," he had said. "I know every inch of this lake."

What he didn't know was that the lake had once extended beyond the beaver dam at the far north corner, and he asked her to show him the house.

As soon as she glimpsed the house through the pine trees, she forgot how big and clumsy she felt. She didn't think, taking off her jeans as she used to so she could wade into the area beneath the house for the boats. Seeing how Kyle watched amusedly from the shore, she felt humiliated, until he, too, was taking off his jeans.

There was only water between them and she wondered whether he expected her to touch him. She didn't know what it was like to really be with someone, and with someone so much older. When she was thirteen, she'd once sneaked into the woods with a boy, and they'd briefly fumbled around in each other's pants before deciding to go for pizza.

Kyle didn't seem to expect anything. Calling out, "Hello!" he seemed equally captivated by the dark echoing space. It wasn't until later when they'd put their jeans back on that he kissed her, tracing the outline of her face so that, for the first time she could ever remember, she felt beautiful.

No one since had made her feel that way. And no one had believed so in her. Maybe she did have a talent for photography, but it was Kyle who had pushed her to her limits. Just when she thought she'd created the best possible composition, he would challenge her to skew the veins in a leaf or the panes in an old Tudor window into even more striking diagonals.

Vickie pulled herself up from the van floor so that she could press her chest against his, so that she could pull him into her.

He kissed her neck and buried his face in her hair. "God, Vickie." He ran his hands around her breasts, gently squeezing her nipples.

She felt herself opening up, and she pushed harder against him, unable to get close enough, as when she used to see him standing at the end of the wharf, one of the places where they would meet after he no longer could risk being seen picking her up after school. Vickie would walk the length of the wharf and when she was finally there, slipping her hands beneath his shirt, she could feel as though she were still walking toward him. Never able to get quite close enough.

CHAPTER 15

$\mathcal{A}$LEX HAD BIKED over to Ruth's again, and Meryl stopped for her on her way to begin setting up at the hall. Ruth seemed particularly agitated, already doing the breakfast dishes. Ordinarily, she wouldn't get around to them until late afternoon.

"Thirty years," Ruth said, gazing through the bottom of a juice glass. "They've been married for thirty years."

"They're only *separating*," Shawna said, sitting on the counter beside the sink. "Depending, I guess, on whether it's only some kind of midlife crisis Mom's going through."

Shawna used to sit like that watching Ruth when she was a little girl, and sometimes she didn't seem to have grown up at all. At the same time, Meryl and Shawna frequently had been calling each other to exchange blender recipes for baby food and advice about frozen bananas for relieving teething pain. Although they hadn't exactly become close friends, Meryl had learned that Phillip liked to pick out Shawna's underwear himself, lace bikini briefs woven loosely so he could glimpse her salamander tattoo. It was hard to imagine Shawna getting a tattoo in the first place, let alone shy Phillip flipping through a Victoria's Secret catalog.

"Did you see this coming?" Meryl asked, pouring a cup of coffee and sitting next to her father at the table.

"Since a couple of years ago when Dad wouldn't pull off the highway to stop at Mom's favorite potter's store. She opened the door anyway, while the car was still moving."

"I don't ever remember a single squabble," Blake said, as Daryll climbed down from his lap. He'd been eyeing the plastic potato scrubber Ruth had knocked to the floor.

"That's it—I don't think they've ever been really honest with each other," Shawna said. "Mom was just so accommodating. This house they so-called built together? She'd hoped for something a little more conventional, something with a few less skylights and domed ceilings. But that's about impossible when you're married to an architect. He talked her out of the smallest things, like the window seat. He wouldn't even allow her that, a window seat."

Vickie came in and sat on the stool in the far corner of the kitchen to nurse a cup of coffee. No one spoke to her. They were used to the way she'd stare bleakly at some spot on the floor until she was fully awake.

Meryl was sure she'd been with Kyle last night, the only reason he wouldn't have been home when he was expecting Meryl. She forced herself to look away from her sister, from the outline of Vickie's legs beneath her oversize T-shirt, the bare skin she could imagine Kyle touching.

"Where's Alex, anyway?" Meryl asked.

"She's out back supervising your uncle cleaning the gutters," Blake said. "He's already fixed the loose board he discovered on the porch steps and the potential leak in the pipe under the bathroom sink."

Meryl looked out the back door. Alex was staring enrapturedly up at Uncle Warren while Phillip held the ladder. Gordon was asleep flat on the deck, a Nerf ball tucked in one elbow.

"Sorry Gordon's so conked out," Shawna said. "I'd wake him for Daryll, but he's been up since five. If I were smart, I'd be napping, too."

"Maybe Aunt Anna just needs to explore her own space for a while," Meryl said. "This friend of mine left her husband to go back to school and get her social worker's degree, but once she'd graduated and opened her own practice, they started dating again. Dating, can you imagine? Three kids and fifteen years of marriage behind them, and they're having little intimate Saturday nights with dinner and a movie."

"So what if they *don't* get back together?" Vickie asked.

They all looked at her as if they'd forgotten she was there.

"They've been married for *thirty years,* Victoria," Ruth said.

"Well, maybe thirty years too long," Vickie said, getting up for a grapefruit.

Ruth looked at Meryl. "Did your sister tell you she's quit her job?"

"She did, Gramma."

"And did you try to talk some sense into her?"

"Yes, Gramma."

"I don't know what she thinks she's doing."

Vickie sat at the table despondently peeling the grapefruit, and Meryl was reminded of how she used to tie those knots in her lunch straws—and of a fact she now couldn't ignore: how much Kyle must still mean to her.

"She's thinking of going to Australia," Meryl said.

"Australia?"

Vickie kicked her gently under the table.

"To live in a cave," Meryl said, and they both laughed.

Ruth frowned, drying her omelette pan until it shone. "We do have grapefruit spoons, you know."

Uncle Warren came into the kitchen and kissed Meryl on the top of her head.

"Sorry about you and Aunt Anna," she said.

"Well, it's all my fault," he said. "Just ask your grandmother who's hardly talking to me."

"I'm talking to you. I just don't understand how you can throw away thirty years of marriage."

"Thirty-one to be exact, Mother."

"I was saying that maybe you two just need time apart," Meryl said. "These friends of mine who divorced and then started dating again finally remarried and had the wedding they'd always wanted, in Atlantic City."

"Thank you, my angel of mercy."

Vickie frowned at Meryl.

"Blake, those gutters look like they haven't been cleaned out since last spring," Uncle Warren said.

"It was the fall, Warren, actually," Blake said evenly. "I cleaned them out just last fall."

Uncle Warren held up his dirt-covered hands. "They were full of decayed leaves."

"There's not a lot we can do about that—it's from that overhanging branch from the maple there."

"We could trim the branch, couldn't we?"

Blake got up then. "I have some things to finish up," he said, and in a moment they heard him going down the basement steps.

"So I hear he's making rat traps now when he's not making toys," Uncle Warren said, examining his hands.

"Rat traps?" Meryl asked.

"We have rats," Vickie said.

"*Rats?* He should be calling the exterminator if we have rats."

"He's seen this work, Meryl," Vickie said.

Meryl knew her father would probably end up having to call the exterminator anyway. The last time he'd tried to solve a problem around the house, he'd taken apart the air conditioner, thinking he could fix it himself as if it were just another lamp.

Uncle Warren laughed. "Rat traps. The kind of thing that drove your mother crazy."

"Well, whatever Blake may tinker with, at least he never would have let his wife go," Ruth said.

Uncle Warren adjusted the faucet toward himself so that Ruth was left clutching the fistful of silverware she'd been about to rinse. "What do you think, Mother. Should we cut off that branch?"

"Your great-grandmother planted that tree in memory of your great-grandfather," Ruth said.

"I didn't say cut the tree down."

"And it was beneath that tree your father proposed to me."

"It was just a thought."

"He told me I was the Holy Grail," Ruth said. "That he'd finally found the Holy Grail."

Uncle Warren dried his hands and swung Daryll onto his shoulders.

"He never would have let *me* go."

"Well, I'm not Father, am I?" Uncle Warren said, leaning side to side so that Daryll giggled. Meryl watched him warily—she knew of a child who'd fallen and cracked his collarbone that way.

Ruth washed the silverware thoroughly instead of putting it in the dishwasher. "And if he were alive, he wouldn't have missed his daughter's funeral."

Uncle Warren lowered Daryll, much to Meryl's relief. "You know, Mother, I realize I seem to be disappointing you. But I don't think it's me you're really angry at anyway. It's Lydia."

"Lydia?"

"The only time *she* ever disappointed you was when she died."

Ruth's mouth fell open a little. She moved toward Uncle Warren, her arms slightly raised as if to embrace him. She slapped him across the face.

Everyone sat in silence, so stunned that even Daryll didn't move from where he'd dropped the potato brush.

Seeming stunned herself, Ruth left the room.

Touching his cheek, Uncle Warren said, "Well, I guess I've really failed to take care of things this time, haven't I?"

He went outside as Phillip came in with Gordon. Phillip looked around at them questioningly, but no one spoke.

From the window Meryl could see Uncle Warren take up a hammer he'd left on the porch. He didn't seem to know what to do with it, finally setting it on the railing like something meant to be displayed.

CHAPTER 16

Ruth actually slapped him." Vickie laughed. "Ruth actually *slapped* Uncle Warren."

"I don't think that's exactly funny," Meryl said, wishing her sister hadn't insisted on coming with her to help at the hall. She opened a package of balloons for Alex to blow up. "Keep them away from your brother," she said, worried that he might try to eat one.

"I know, I know, it's not funny. Just surprising. *Very* surprising."

"What do you think, should the band set up here?" Meryl asked, moving over to one corner. "They're going to play some of those songs Ruth would crank up, you know, like 'Whispering,' re-member? Her favorite—she always had some story about some young man courting her to go along with it."

"So is this going to be some kind of time warp?"

"Well, what should they play, the Rolling Stones? Maybe I'll set up the presents on a table over there—"

"All these people are bringing presents?"

"It's a *birthday*, Vickie. And I thought I'd have her open them after everyone's seated at the tables eating. Then afterward, a short interlude of music and dancing while I get the cake ready. And then I'll bring it out while the band's playing 'Happy Birthday'—"

"You've got this pretty well orchestrated, haven't you?"

"Can't you say one positive thing?" Meryl asked, handing Vickie the pink paper tablecloths. "And don't put them on any old way. Make sure the edges are even."

"So do you think Gramma's ever done that be-fore?" Vickie asked.

"Done what?" Meryl asked distractedly, trying to decide where to set up the buffet table.

"Slap him. Slap Uncle Warren."

"All I know is, I hope they get along for the party."

"Is that all you can think about, this party?"

"Yes, Vickie, as a matter of fact it is. After all this work, I want Ruth to have a good time, okay? Although why she had to go and provoke Uncle Warren like that, I don't know, make him say something he'll regret."

"How do you know he regrets it?" Vickie asked.

"It was a pretty cruel thing to say, don't you think?"

"Well, maybe there's some truth in it."

"Don't tell me you're actually sticking up for your poor old Uncle Warren."

"Well, when *do* you think Mom ever disappointed Gramma?"

"She wouldn't *want* to—they were too close for that."

"And what makes you sure they were so close, anyway?"

"Do you have to question absolutely everything?"

"Just because she never had the guts to stand up to Gramma?"

"Stand up for *what?*"

"Anything. She never stood up for anything. Not even when I was so late for my piano recital, I missed the beginning of the first piece."

"Recital? What recital?"

"You were there . . . ," Vickie said, feeling a little embarrassed now for bringing up something so far in the past. "Anyway, it was because of Gramma. And it was Gramma who put all that fear into her head about my going off by myself to the desert, cutting out articles about rattlesnakes. Always cutting out articles, even about poultry."

"Mom had some reason to be nervous, Vickie."

"Maybe some. But maybe it was something she actually wanted to do herself."

Meryl laughed. "Mom going to the desert?"

"Gail thinks Mom and I were actually alike."

Trying not to sound surprised, Meryl said, "Well, only if in some way I don't know about you."

"Or about her."

Meryl was getting tired of this. "Since when does Gail know so much, anyway? She's so preoccupied with those dogs, taking them everywhere, even shopping when she has to leave them locked up in the car. They're so big and wild—"

"They're not wild," Alex said, from where she sat cross-legged surrounded by balloons. "Just big."

"They were best friends, Mel," Vickie said.

"And I never understood that."

"Exactly," Vickie said.

"Exactly what?"

"Anything's possible."

Meryl said to Alex, who was clearly paying too

close attention, "Honey, can you run out for me? There's that package of streamers I left in the car."

"I won't listen. . . ."

"Go on, all right?"

Alex took a balloon with her, and when she'd left, Meryl said, "You know, this has more to do with you than it has anything to do with Mom, this obsession of yours."

"What obsession?"

"Come on."

"Why can't anyone just say it? Suicide."

"Because it doesn't apply."

"Doesn't *apply?* What is it, some job requirement?"

"It's no one's fault you two didn't get along, Victoria."

"I didn't say it was—you think I'm feeling guilty?"

"Are you?"

"You just said I have nothing to be guilty about."

"You don't. But why else are you thinking so much about it?"

"Well, you seem to be thinking about it, too— you're the one who brought it up," Vickie said.

"I didn't bring it up. . . ."

"You did, Meryl. All *I* said was anything's possible."

Meryl looked out the window to see what was

taking Alex so long. She was tossing the balloon, and Meryl was glad for an excuse to go outside.

The fact was, Meryl had been thinking about it and more than she cared to. She'd been remembering her mother's way of gazing vacantly, when she could seem farther away than when she'd lose Meryl and Vickie in a crowd. One night when Meryl was thirteen, she'd come down to find her mother sitting at the dining-room table emptying a piggy bank. Lydia looked at Meryl in that vacant way, and she said, "Twenty years' worth of pennies. He'd been saving pennies for twenty years."

The bank had been given to her by an old man with terminal cancer she'd been reading to as part of a volunteer program at the nursing home, and Meryl knew the man must have died since her mother was home unusually early.

Lydia ran her fingers through the pennies, and Meryl felt suddenly uneasy; her mother seemed so different. Different from when she would nervously fuss so with her hair. Even different from when she was showing a house after picking Meryl up from dance class, when she'd move with such confidence through the empty rooms, her heels clattering emphatically across the wood floors.

To get her mother to look at her, Meryl asked, "So are you going to spend them?"

"No, honey. I couldn't do that." Lydia swept the pennies into a pile. "You should be in bed."

Meryl sat there a moment longer, relieved that her mother was brushing the pennies into the bottom of the bank as she would brush crumbs off the table.

Meryl hadn't thought much about the bank back then, but now she remembered her mother didn't even like the man, and she wondered what the bank had meant to her, what she really had been thinking as she spread those pennies out across the table.

And how often she'd wondered that—what her mother was thinking. Even when Meryl was relating some funny incident about the kids or complaining about work, Lydia sometimes would gaze at Meryl as she used to gaze out the window on those full moon nights when she'd take Vickie and Meryl up to the third floor where they could see how the ocean was silver through the tips of the trees. When she didn't have to focus on anything in particular and there was only that open space.

"Vickie accuses *me* of being panoramic," Meryl was saying to Glenn that night, as she was getting into bed. "But she's driving herself nuts, the way she has to examine everything under a microscope."

Just out of the shower, Glenn was towel-drying his hair. "Panoramic?"

"For being too fair. How can you be too fair?

Meanwhile, she's never given me any credit for how I've always supported her. Every time she and Mom came to blows, I was the one mediating."

"Mediating isn't exactly supporting."

Meryl looked at the familiar knobs of his spine as he held his head bent. She used to enjoy gently kneading them with her fingertips after making love.

"I'm not trying to challenge you," he said.

"I was the one to convince our mother photography was what Vickie really wanted to do when she dropped out of college. I was the one to convince her to let Vickie move back home for that internship at the *Gazette*."

"Well, what about Kyle?"

For something to do, Meryl rubbed on more hand cream from the jar she kept on the bedside table. "What about him?"

"Would you say you were being exactly supportive then?"

"Vickie was only sixteen—he wasn't good for her."

"He was important to her." Glenn got into bed and turned out the light. "All I'm saying is, maybe Vickie was getting from him a kind of real support she wasn't getting at home."

"*Real* support?"

He rolled onto his stomach and slid his hands beneath his pillow, the way he fell asleep every night.

"Come on, Mel. You've never tried to really understand her."

"All I did was try to understand her, try to figure out why she did half the things she did."

"See?" he said, laughing. "You're still as critical of her as your mother was."

Meryl sat up and looked at him in the dark. "Do you wish you'd married my sister instead?"

"*What?*"

"Then why do you keep sticking up for her—over the party and now this?"

He buried his face in his pillow.

"Do you?"

"Do I what?"

"Do you wish it was her you met at the mall instead of me?"

"You're being really childish now, you know that."

She did know that, but she couldn't help herself. "*Do* you?"

"No, I *don't*. But you know what I do wish? I wish I knew what was really going on."

"What's going on? Nothing's going on."

He turned on the light. "Nothing?"

He searched her face, and she had to look away. She didn't remember ever having to look away from him. Not even when she'd been lying about going out with the girls.

Nodding, he got out of bed.

"Where are you going?" she asked, a new terror ripping through her.

He didn't answer as he put on his bathrobe.

In a moment she heard the television being turned on. She lay flat on her back rubbing her palms against the sheets until they burned, wanting to go to him. If she did go, she'd tell him the rest of what he seemed already to have figured out. She felt as sick to her stomach as she would looking down from the smallest height, like standing on the bed to dust cobwebs from the ceiling. She closed her eyes but felt herself losing her balance. She tried to focus on one stationary object, the stuffed Easter bunny that Glenn had given her back in high school and that she'd always kept on their bureau. She listened to that tinny, faraway sound of canned laughter, until she heard a live gunshot.

She ran outside. The dog had landed on its side and quickly grew still. Meryl knew it was dead. In the porch light, she could see that it was one of Gail's dogs. It was Clara.

CHAPTER 17

CLARA LAY on her side with her legs stretched taut. She'd been shot in the chest and her diamond of white was streaked with blood.

"How could you do it?" asked Vickie, who had come over after Meryl called. "How could you actually do it?"

"Christ." Glenn didn't seem to hear her. He was circling the dog. "Christ."

"I didn't even know you had one. That you really had a gun."

"It's always hung on our wall," Meryl said. "From his father, that old conversation piece . . ."

"But how? How could you shoot someone's dog?"

"He didn't know it was Gail's," Meryl said, digging her nails into the deflated soccer ball that had been lying out on their lawn since Christmas. "He wasn't think—"

"Shut up, Meryl! You can just shut up!"

"*Glenn!*" Vickie had never heard him yell at her sister.

"It's all right," Meryl said with a quietness that surprised Vickie. She let the ball drop and gently cradled it between her feet. "Really."

Alex came outside.

"No, honey," Meryl said, holding her back. "You don't need to see this."

Alex looked past her. "It's Clara."

"Let's go inside."

"Clara's dead?" she asked, sounding not at all older and wiser now, but young and fragile.

"It was an accident. . . ." Meryl said, her voice trailing off as she gently nudged Alex back toward the house. Both went inside, Alex looking back over her shoulder as she started to cry.

"Christ." Glenn took off his glasses to rub his eyes. "I have to tell Gail."

"She'll want to see her," Vickie said. "She'll probably want her buried in her yard."

Without his glasses, his eyes were as small as Ruth's.

"I'll go with you," Vickie said, less out of any compassion for Glenn than for Gail.

He nodded, looking relieved. "I'll get a tarp."

Left alone with Clara, Vickie felt compelled to kneel for a closer look. The blood had begun to congeal; her diamond was darkened to a muddy brown. But in the porch light, her black coat shimmered with blue. And Vickie could glimpse her teeth, coated with tartar around the gums, but pearl white at their tips. A film lightened her brown eyes to a rich caramel.

Vickie stroked her ears. Although cold now, they were still smooth as silk, something that restored a faith Vickie hadn't known she'd lost; she felt suddenly filled, as if she'd taken a long drink of something not sweet but the least bit tangy and warm.

Gail tentatively lifted a corner of the tarp in the back of Glenn's truck, ignoring the other two dogs barking from inside and leaping against the screen door.

She cocked her head, considering Clara, running her fingers back and forth along the tarp the way Vickie had seen her indulge in the feel of her fabrics. She was wearing only her nightgown and her hair fell across her face. Vickie couldn't remember whether she'd ever seen Gail's hair down before and found herself wondering how tangled it must be by morning.

Glenn leaned both hands on the truck, his head hanging between his arms. He traced the inside of the hubcap with the toe of his boot. "I'm sorry. Really sorry . . ."

Gail replaced the corner of the tarp carefully tucking it around Clara.

"It doesn't look like there was any pain," Vickie said, trying to think of something, anything, to say.

Gail brushed away seeds dropping onto the tarp from the apple tree. "You can bury her out back, by the rhododendron." She went inside the house. Vickie followed her.

The other two dogs filled Gail's living room, their tails knocking against the coffee table, rattling the ceramic bowl of marble eggs.

"The place is a mess," Gail said, although everything was in its proper place as it always had been. She adjusted the afghan draped across one of the love seats.

"Are you okay?" Vickie asked.

"I'm fine, dear."

"You have a right to be upset, Gail."

"I'll make you some tea."

"You don't need to make tea," Vickie said, alarmed by how calm she seemed. Gail ignored her and went into the kitchen.

It had been some time since Vickie had been over there. Gail seemed always to be coming by Ruth's now, no matter how difficult it was for the two of them to get along. But before her mother died, Vickie knew she still often spent her afternoons at Gail's house. She imagined that they had sat over a tray of tea in the alcove as they used to on those afternoons when her father first gave up law.

Vickie had liked having that excuse to come over after school so that she could swing on Ray's tire. One afternoon, there was a dark bottle on the tray, and when Vickie went out back to swing on the tire, she could see her mother through the window pouring some of whatever was in the bottle into her tea. Vickie swung higher and higher trying not to think about the night before when her father confessed to having turned down an offer to sell vacuums door-to-door. "You really want to see me become some kind of Avon Lady?" he'd asked. "I want to see you become *something!*" Lydia had yelled.

When they finally left Gail's that afternoon, Vickie's mother weaved her way up through the woods until she stumbled and fell. Laughing, she threw a fistful of leaves at Vickie, and Vickie threw a fistful back. It had been some time since they'd had such fun together, at least not since her father dissolved the firm.

But then Gail appeared. As if Lydia had been expecting her, she lay back, sweeping her arms through the leaves. "I had a feeling . . . ," Gail said, helping her up. Lydia leaned her head on Gail's shoulder as Gail helped her the rest of the way home through the woods. Vickie hadn't realized then that her mother was "drunk," what her father called her when he was taking her upstairs.

From Gail's alcove window, Vickie could see Glenn out by the rhododendron, and she wondered whether she should be helping. But she didn't feel much like being around him.

Gail came back in with a tray of tea, and they sat in the alcove. They didn't speak until Glenn was lowering Clara into the hole, and Gail said, "I loved her, Vickie."

"I know."

"No. I mean your mother." Gail pulled all her hair around so that she could twist the ends. "I loved her . . . ," she said quietly. It was the stillness of a violence that could only erupt from within, could be felt like a single tremor from deep within the earth, and Vickie suddenly remembered when she had once before seen Gail's hair down.

It was on an afternoon sometime after she'd found Gail and her mother drinking from that dark bottle together. They were sitting out on the grass, and both had their blouses unbuttoned and skirts pulled up to get a tan, Vickie thought. Her mother held her face up to the sun, and Vickie hadn't thought much then about the fact that Gail lay with her head in her mother's lap. About the way her mother was running her fingers through Gail's hair stretched out into a train across the grass.

She wondered now if they'd been drinking then too. She wished she could remember seeing that dark bottle again, something to explain why they had been sitting like that.

The dogs had settled beneath the table and they leaned heavily against Vickie's legs. She was aware suddenly of how strongly they smelled. "Maybe Glenn needs help," she said, needing to be outside.

PART TWO

CHAPTER 18

BY THE TIME Vickie and her father
drove Ruth to the party, the hall was
filled. "Who *are* they? Who are all
these people?" Ruth asked, plucking at the corsage
Meryl had given her, looking as bewildered as when
Vickie took her to Rockefeller Center the one time
she ever visited New York.

Ill at ease around crowds, Blake was already loos-
ening his tie. "Well, there's Helen Dixon and Jacob
Thomas—"

"Of course, but what about the rest? Who are all the rest of these people?"

"Well, I think that's Mrs. Shultz, over by the buffet table. . . ."

"Mrs. Shultz? From the dry cleaners?"

Ruth looked increasingly bewildered as her friends and more-or-less acquaintances began to surround her, and Vickie knew then how much her grandmother really didn't want this party. She'd known when Ruth had taken so long to get ready, and Vickie had finally gone upstairs. Ruth was all dressed and sitting by her window, her hands open, palms-up on her knees, the way she'd sat after the reception following Lydia's service. When all had been done that needed to be done. When she had even picked out the crumbs from the carpet and there was nothing left to do but fully feel Lydia's absence.

"*There* she is!" Meryl exclaimed, balancing a couple of hors d'oeuvre platters as she made her way through the throng. She would have looked particularly demure in her off-white dress with the lace sailor collar if it hadn't been for the deep neckline and her curled hair falling across one eye. And how revived and fresh she seemed, considering how she had stood last night over Clara's body, digging her nails into the deflated ball.

Vickie herself couldn't shake the image of that white diamond stained with blood, an image surreal against the backdrop of pink tablecloths, balloons, and streamers. There had been the final glint of Clara's pearl-white teeth in the light from Gail's window before Vickie and Glenn were patting down the last shovelfuls of dirt. The ground was only slightly raised to suggest that it had been disturbed at all, and Vickie had felt a loss not so much for Clara as for that moment of feeling filled when she'd stroked her ears.

"What *took* her so long?" Meryl whispered to Vickie. "The party was supposed to start at seven." Before Vickie could answer, she said, "And everyone knows already."

"Knows what?"

"About the dog. Mrs. Richards is all fireworks tonight."

"Well, people have to have something to talk about."

"Gail didn't have to tell Mrs. Richards—she knows as well as anyone news with her travels faster than the *Gazette*."

"You think Gail's probably thinking about that right now?"

Meryl's mouth froze into a tight smile as someone plucked a carrot stick from one of the platters.

"Maybe she wants people to know," Vickie said.

"For what? To punish Glenn?"

"He did shoot her dog, Meryl."

"I know he shot her dog. Everyone knows, okay? Everyone knows my husband shot Gail's dog. I've got some pigs-in-a-blanket in the oven; go check on them, will you? Gail insists on helping out, but every time I go in there she's walking in circles."

Gail was moving back and forth across the kitchen, picking things up and putting them down as Ruth would. Alex sat on the counter poking holes with a plastic fork through the bottom of a paper cup.

"I don't know how Meryl's managed to stay so organized, doing virtually all this herself," Gail said.

Just as they were beginning to burn, Vickie took the pigs-in-a-blanket out of the oven.

"Oh, dear, I forgot. There's so much to remember. . . ." Gail peered into the refrigerator without taking anything out. There were dark, puffy shadows beneath her eyes.

"You don't look like you got any sleep at all," Vickie said.

"Oh, well . . . I'm not sure how exactly they can know, but Mindy and Sage wouldn't settle down."

"Dogs can sense those things, sometimes better than humans," Vickie said, arranging the pigs-in-a-blanket on a platter. "They speak a different language, that's all."

"And they can see things we can't see," Alex said, holding up two cups like a pair of binoculars. "They can see things miles away—Clara was always looking up at the trees."

"She was their leader, the way they'd tag along after her . . . ," Gail said, following her own train of thought as she opened the refrigerator again. In the flaxen yellow light she looked jaundiced, her gaze traveling from one shelf to another. "She had a particular instinct, intelligence. I mean, I've never known very much about dogs. I've never known very much about anything, for that matter. But I did know about her. I knew she was special. Well, special to me—"

"What are you looking for?" Meryl asked, carrying in some empty platters.

Gail glanced around at the entire kitchen. "Well, now I forget."

Vickie had never seen Gail so scattered. Not even at the reception after the memorial service when she had been the one most capable of remembering to pass the hors d'oeuvres. Not even last night when she'd been able to make tea.

"Alex, all the other kids are out playing, why don't you go join them," Meryl said.

Alex stabbed her fork into the bottom of another cup.

Frowning, Meryl turned to Vickie. "They're

getting cold," she said, pointing at the pigs-in-a-blanket.

Ordinarily, Ruth's friends from the club looked at Vickie curiously, unable to disassociate her from the little girl notorious for intentionally tripping her partners during waltzing classes. But as she passed them the hors d'oeuvres, they were most interested in the dog, as were Ruth's friends from the church, who usually stared at Vickie with furrowed brows as if she still could be caught skipping confirmation class to run in and out among the pews in the darkened chapel.

"How could he do it? How could he shoot her dog?" asked Ginger Markson, who had both arms in casts from too many years of needlepointing.

"He didn't know it was Gail's dog," Vickie said.

"But how could he shoot *any* dog?"

Even those people Vickie didn't recognize were asking her about Clara, the ones with whom Ruth probably "talked up a storm," the little balding man with flour on his shoes as if he'd come directly from making pizzas at Dolphin's, and a couple of other men Vickie vaguely remembered from their having been at Ruth's to fix the clogged tub drain, or maybe it was a leak in the roof. She glanced over at Glenn who was tending bar, at how he kept his head lowered to avert the stares. As she made her way through the crowd, she kept a constant lookout for Kyle.

The band was playing swing tunes to which mostly Ruth's generation was dancing, although a few of the younger were trying to adapt their own free-styles. Including Vickie's uncle.

"Since when does your father dance?" she asked Shawna.

"He's had a couple of scotches," Shawna said, trying to keep Gordon from yanking the paper cloths off the tables.

"I didn't know he drank either."

"He doesn't. At least he didn't before all this. And how about your father?"

"Dad?"

"Who's the woman in green? You can't miss her—a bright emerald."

Vickie had never seen her father dance with anyone besides her mother, Lydia having been the only one able to drag him out onto the floor. And since she died, Vickie hadn't seen him look so animated, gesticulating with one hand and leaning toward the woman in green, trying to talk above the music.

Gail was standing against the counter twisting her braid when Vickie returned her platters to the kitchen. Alex was poking holes through the bottom of another cup.

"Do you know who the woman in the green dress is? Dad's dancing with her."

"Woman in green?"

"She doesn't look like she's from around here."

"I don't know any woman in green," Gail said, restacking the empty hors d'oeuvre platters, the only thing left to do since Meryl had already arranged the food on the buffet table.

Alex was aligning her perforated cups into a neat row, and Vickie asked, "You going to save any for the guests?"

"There are *plenty*. There are thousands and thousands of cups," Alex said, sounding as distracted as Gail.

"You know, there's Gail's spaghetti casserole out there," Vickie said.

"With cheese?"

"Plenty of cheese."

Alex reluctantly climbed down from the counter.

When she'd left, Vickie said to Gail, "You don't have to stay in here all night either."

"They may need more food, forks, knives—"

"You don't have to play caterer."

"Look, I don't feel like having to listen to anyone else tell me how sorry they are."

"They are sorry."

"Oh, no, they're not. They're just interested in how a perfectly nice person like Glenn could go and shoot a dog."

"I think he does feel bad about it, Gail."

"Of course he does. But that won't bring Clara back, will it?"

"*This* won't bring back Clara either."

Vickie had to leave the kitchen, unable to bear Gail's questioning look. Confused herself as to why she'd suddenly lost patience, she headed for the bar. She was missing Kyle terribly now.

"You haven't seen Kyle, have you?" she asked Glenn.

"Kyle? No, only about everyone else in this town."

"You want some relief?"

"Thanks, but no thanks. I think I'm safer behind the bar."

"It will pass, you know."

"Maybe. But maybe not with Gail."

"She doesn't have a perspective right now."

"And why should she?" he said sadly, and Vickie began to feel a little sorry for him.

"This has become like some damn political rally," Uncle Warren said, coming over to the bar.

"Maybe you've had enough, what do you say?" Glenn asked.

"I say another round," he said, handing Glenn his glass. "So your grandmother doesn't look like she's having a very good time, does she?"

"I don't even see her."

"She's retreated to that far table where no one else can find her either." Glenn handed him his drink.

"Of course, that has more to do with me than anyone else."

"What does?"

"Her not having a good time."

"She's just upset about you and Aunt Anna."

"She's not upset with Anna; she's upset with me. It's *me*," he said, jiggling his ice so that his drink splattered.

"Well, maybe you should be talking to her about that," Vickie said, starting to walk away from him.

Catching up with her, he asked, "Why do you hate me so much?"

Vickie was surprised at how pathetic he suddenly seemed. "I don't hate you."

He took out his watch, checking the time, and she was relieved. But pausing to weigh it on his palm, he said, "You know, it was three days before Father died when he gave me this. I sat on his bed and he pressed it into my hand. He pressed it so hard it hurt." Uncle Warren turned over the watch to trace the engraved initials. "He made me promise to always take care of my mother and sister. I was twelve." He slipped the watch back into his pocket. *"Twelve."*

Vickie had never heard this story before, and she tried to imagine him as a little boy sitting on his father's bed like that. She couldn't and said, "I'm going to go keep Gramma company."

"What are you doing by yourself?"

Ruth poked at her food. "There's hardly anyone here I know."

"Well, that's a bit of an exaggeration. Besides, that's never stopped you."

"You'd think nothing else happens in this town the way everyone's talking about that dog."

"Nothing else does happen."

"And look at your uncle."

Uncle Warren was back on the dance floor. Dancing with no one in particular, he was moving in circles as sparrows would sometimes flounder around on Vickie's fire escape after flying into her windowpane.

"Do you know who that is Daddy's been dancing with?"

"I told you, I don't know anyone," Ruth said irritably.

"Here you are," Gail said, bringing over her own plate. She smiled a pleasant but strained smile, and Vickie realized how trying it was for her to have finally surfaced from the kitchen.

"Anyway, what woman?" Ruth asked offhandedly, trying to conceal any real curiosity.

"Over there, in the bright emerald dress."

"That *is* bright," Ruth said.

"Oh, I guess I do remember her," Gail said. "Catherine something, I forget her last name. She came over about some chairs that needed new covers."

"She's not from around here, is she?"

"From Chicago. Bought up the old Crest place to convert into a restaurant."

"Ruth, everyone's been wondering where you disappeared to," Ginger Markson said, coming over accompanied by the Fremonts, also from the church.

She sat down, touching Gail's arm. "Oh, I'm so sorry, really—"

"It was an accident," Gail said as mechanically as if she were reciting an overrehearsed line.

"Honestly, I didn't know Glenn had it in him. . . ."

Gail twisted the end of her braid.

"Well, accidents do happen," Ruth said.

Gail clamped her mouth shut so that her cheekbones jutted sharply.

"Maybe it's not that simple, Gramma," Vickie said.

"That it was an accident?" Ruth asked innocently. "Of course, it was an accident. He didn't know it was Gail's."

"All the same, he shot to kill," Mr. Fremont said.

His wife poked him.

"Well, it's not like his target was a squirrel."

"My grandson-in-law wouldn't shoot to kill," Ruth said.

"He hit her squarely in the chest," Gail said, leaning across the table. Her dress seemed too big for her, slipping off one shoulder so that her bra strap showed, and she seemed as thin and gaunt as if she were dwindling away right there in front of them. "He didn't have to hit her squarely in the chest."

Ruth was about to say something, but then Meryl was taking her by the hand and leading her away to open her presents.

Ruth's head barely showed above the pile of gifts, and Vickie was reminded of how she had to keep her chin lifted to see over the dashboard of her Thunderbird. Meryl had set up a microphone on the table, and she craned it toward Ruth so that the crinkling of paper reverberated like thunder as Ruth began unwrapping the smallest box.

"You have to tell us who they're from, Gramma," Meryl said into the microphone.

Putting on her bifocals to peer at the card, Ruth said as faintly as if she'd never before spoken into a microphone as she had often done while rallying support for her various causes, "A Mr. Lee."

"Oh, Mr. Lee, of course, Gramma, that explains the cow at the end of the key chain—'Lee's Dairy.'"

There were other presents similar to the key chain, from people who couldn't have known Ruth well enough to give anything more personal. As she waded through the pile, Ruth's eyes became as glazed as if she'd retreated into some cool shady area of herself, and Vickie was reminded of all those interminable Sweet Sixteen parties when the birthday girl could look equally bored, seated alone at a table with a microphone. People had begun to get up and mill about, picking at whatever food was left on the buffet.

Finally, Ruth reached the bottom of the pile. "Thank you, each and every one of you," she said, slinking back to her table with unusual shyness.

Meryl had signaled for the band to start playing again, and Ginger said, "Ruth, it's 'Whispering,' remember?"

"I remember," Ruth said dully.

Uncle Warren weaved toward them. "Mother, I can't believe you're not out there doing the foxtrot."

"Yes, why don't you go dance with your son?" Ginger said.

"I'm not as limber as I used to be."

"Just because it's your birthday is no reason to start feeling your age, Gramma," Vickie said.

"Yes, listen to your granddaughter," Ginger said, drifting off toward the dance floor.

"Why am I always being told to listen to my granddaughter?"

"Maybe because she has something to say," Gail said.

Ruth frowned.

"Come on, Mother, do me the honor," Uncle Warren said. Losing his balance, he caught himself on the table.

"You're making a fool of yourself."

"A fool?"

"You're drunk, Warren."

"I am, aren't I? I'm *out of control*. What do you think of that, Mother?"

"Are you trying to embarrass me?"

"Yes, Mother, I'm specifically making a fool of myself to embarrass you."

"Well then, this maybe has something to do with why Anna's leaving in the first place."

"Because I'm a fool?"

"Because you're thinking only of yourself."

"*I'm* thinking only of myself?" Shaking his head, he walked off.

Ruth fingered her bifocals hooked into her collar. "Oh, he won't listen. Why won't he listen?"

"Why won't you?" Gail asked.

Ruth looked fixedly at Gail.

"Well, don't you think he's as unhappy about all this as you are?"

"You always have something to add, don't you?"

"If I do, it's because you won't let anyone else get a word in edgewise."

Ruth daintily dabbed at the corners of her mouth with her crumpled pink napkin. "You know, I'm sorry about Clara. I mean, if it were my poor old Piper . . . But I don't think that gives you license to say whatever you please."

"*You* say whatever you please."

"Don't you think you're overreacting just a little bit?"

"Well, you *won't* listen, Ruth."

"I don't mean Warren; I mean about Clara—you're clearly distraught."

Gail gazed down at the full plate she'd hardly touched as Vickie had seen her gaze down Ruth's old well.

"I know she was important to you—" Ruth began.

"You don't know."

"All right then, I don't know. All I do know is that everyone's talking about it, and at my party."

"Well, I apologize for that, for interfering with your neat little scheme of things."

Those red spots began to break out on Ruth's cheeks. "She was a *dog*, Gail."

"She was *Clara*. Can't you get that?" Vickie said.

By the way Ruth's corsage trembled, Vickie could see her breath quickening with anger.

"It's all right, Vickie," Gail said.

"It's not all right," Ruth said. "She's always been like this."

"Leave her alone, Ruth."

"Leave her alone? Yes, that was always your idea, anyway, always letting her off the hook. Every time Lydia tried to show some discipline, you'd say, 'Leave her alone, leave her alone.' "

"That wasn't Lydia, that was you. Everything had to be a lesson."

"Well, how else do you think children learn except from lessons?"

"From experience, plain old experience."

"Stealing is an experience?"

"I more than learned my lesson," Vickie said. She'd been caught trying to steal a hand radio, and instead of reporting her to the police, the store manager had her stock shelves without pay for three months.

"You even stole from your own mother," Ruth said.

Vickie looked away from her grandmother's eyes, now more piercing than beady.

"That wasn't shoplifting, that was something else," Gail said. "And Lydia knew it. Like she knew there's a reason a kid decides to take off on a bus by herself. Something they can't always explain. Not even to their own mother."

"She knew that?" Vickie asked.

"It was wrong," Ruth said. "She had to learn right from wrong."

"And whose idea was that?" Gail asked.

"I don't have to listen to this."

"No, you won't listen to anyone," Gail said. "Not even your own son."

"My son? Why don't you look at *your* son, for goodness' sake—where is he now?"

Gail grew quiet for a moment, looking out at the dance floor. "That was his father."

"And you should have left him years ago."

"Don't you think I know that?"

"Then who are you to talk?"

"Whatever's become of Ray, I let him go," Gail said. "You never let Lydia go. And now you won't let go of Warren."

"Let her *go?*" Ruth began to shake as she hadn't since Gail insisted Lydia would have wanted her ashes scattered in the ocean. "And what do you know about that? You only know about losing a *goddamn dog.*"

Vickie had never heard her grandmother swear before. She felt as though the three of them were shrouded within a heavy, dark tent.

"I loved her, too, Ruth," Gail said quietly. "You know, I loved her too."

"She wasn't your daughter!"

"She was *everything*." Gail pressed a fist into her stomach as if she were in pain. "She became . . . everything," she said, with that same violent quietness Vickie remembered from last night when they'd watched Glenn lower Clara into the hole, when Vickie had first recalled having seen Gail with her hair down.

Seeming to sense that violence herself, Ruth lifted one hand to her face as if she now were the one who'd been slapped. She got up and rather staggeringly headed in the direction of Blake.

"You can't leave," Vickie said, catching up with Ruth, knowing that she was going to ask him to drive her home.

"You're not feeling well?" Blake asked. Ruth had torn him away from the woman in green.

"I'm tired."

"You're not tired," Vickie said.

"And I've had about enough of your disrespect."

The band started playing "Happy Birthday," and Vickie knew Meryl was about to bring out the cake. "Don't do this to her, Gramma. Don't do this to Meryl."

Ruth looked around for a moment as though she actually might change her mind but then said, "Oh, this party isn't for me, anyway, dear," her voice diminishing as when she'd been opening her presents. "It's for her. She did this for herself."

Ruth slipped quickly out the back door by the kitchen before anyone could notice she was gone. Blake followed reluctantly.

Meryl had set the cake on the buffet table, and for a long moment, Vickie could only gape at how uncomfortable she seemed peering around for Ruth, fussing with her sailor collar. Vickie made her way through the crowd.

"She left, Meryl."

"Left? What do you mean left?"

"She was . . . tired."

"Tired? She was *tired?*" Meryl said, now wringing her collar like a dishrag. "How could she? How could she leave?"

Vickie couldn't remember her sister so at a loss. "You should probably make some kind of announcement, Mel."

"Saying what? Sorry but the birthday girl's decided to leave her own party?" Her lipstick had worn off, leaving only the peach shadow of her liner so that she looked pale and tired.

"Sorry, Mel," Vickie said.

"Oh, Gramma's just being Gramma."

"She's not. She's being obstinate."

"She's being *Gramma*. She's being *Ruth*. Ruth, Ruth, *Ruth!*" Meryl spit. She blew out the candles herself and began to cut the cake. "Here. You love chocolate," she said, shoving the edge of a cake plate into Vickie's chest.

The chocolate smeared onto Vickie's dress, and Vickie hated her then. She hated her for irritably trying to wipe off the chocolate herself as if it had been Vickie who made the mess.

"And your boyfriend's looking for you," Meryl said, nodding in the direction of the bar.

Kyle had just gotten himself a beer. "He's not my boyfriend, Meryl."

"Then what the hell is he?" Meryl asked.

Vickie tossed her cake into the garbage. "I didn't even want any. Why didn't you ask first if I even wanted any?"

She went over to Kyle, leaving her sister to face the crowd now gathering around the buffet table, asking where Ruth had gone.

"What's this rumbling about Ruth having left?" Kyle asked.

"The rumbling's right."

"How could she leave her own party?"

"I don't know." Vickie didn't want to be thinking about Gail, about the way she'd held her fist against her stomach. And she didn't want to be feeling sorry for her sister who was cutting the cake into smaller and smaller pieces as if she were making surgical incisions.

"Let's go to the beach."

"I just got here," Kyle said.

"I don't care."

"Fine," he said, sounding relieved.

As they were leaving, three boys of about high-school age whom Vickie didn't think had been invited in the first place were causing a commotion at the bar.

"You think we can't fuckin' hold our liquor?" the one in a Grateful Dead jacket yelled. Glenn was refusing to serve him along with the other two boys.

Meryl came over clutching her cake knife.

"And what, you going to hurt me with your big blade?" He laughed.

Glenn grabbed the boy by his shoulders, knocking over some liquor bottles as he pulled him across the table. "Go home to your mothers, *now!*"

Anyone who'd been standing near enough to witness this scene turned to stare not at the boys but at Glenn.

The band had stopped playing, and the hall grew utterly quiet.

The boys lingered a moment longer, twitching nervously. They left, trying to keep their stride.

Glenn looked around at the people staring at him. "That's it, I'm closing up the bar."

"You can't," Meryl said. "Look at all the people still here."

"Meryl, the *birthday girl* isn't even here," he said, piling the liquor bottles back into their boxes.

There was a crash. Gordon had tugged on the buffet tablecloth so that the rest of the cake fell. He crouched in the middle of it, digging his hands into the icing.

Meryl stared at the mess as if not quite seeing it.

"Come on," Vickie whispered, taking Kyle's hand, needing to be outside as she had last night when Gail's dogs had smelled so strongly, leaning against her legs.

"No stars tonight," Vickie said when they were parked at the beach.

"It's so clear, you can see the dipper."

"You know what I mean."

Glenn nodded. "Tide's too low." He draped his hands through the steering wheel, and she knew this time he had no intention of touching her.

"Are you in love with her? This woman you're seeing?"

"In love with her? No, I'm not in love with her."

"Then what?"

He took his hands out of the steering wheel but only to rap his knuckles against the window glass. "Come on, Vickie, we don't need to be talking about this."

"I'm just wondering . . . well, what it is."

"What what is?"

"Between you and her." Vickie didn't know she could sound so jealous.

"Forget about her, all right?"

She looked out the window. She could see the tree from which Kyle had picked the peaches for the basket he'd given her mother. Its fruit was still hard and green.

"She has nothing to do with us, Vickie."

"There isn't an us."

"That was your decision."

"Why do you keep reminding me of that?"

He took the broken comb from the dashboard and plucked at its few remaining teeth.

"What would I have done here, Kyle? What's for me here?"

"Is there anything for you *anywhere?*"

She looked at him, unable to remember his sounding so exasperated with her.

"I'm just beginning to wonder . . . God, Vickie, I don't know. I mean, maybe that *is* it—you just like the idea of a big black hole."

"Don't . . ." She couldn't bear that he might be losing faith. Not so much in them, but in her.

He touched her hair. "I'm sorry." He put his arm around her, and she reached up to kiss him.

"Don't, sweetie."

She moved her hand to his crotch. "It's all right. I'm all right with this," she said.

"No."

She slipped her hand beneath his shirt. She stroked his chest until he pulled her hand back down to his crotch.

In the back of the van, he reached around to unzip her dress, and she thought he'd pull it off so that he could run his hands along her body. He pulled down the dress only as far as her shoulders and rolled down her pantyhose. He pushed aside her panties and entered her. He went at her with a ferocity less passionate than impatient, and she thought she could actually feel the streetlight filtering through the plaid curtains, so cold it burned like ice against her bare arms. She saw Gail again. She saw her holding her fist against her stomach. She saw her hair down, the way she had lain on the grass with her head in her mother's lap.

Kyle became still. She'd never known him to come so quickly and so quietly. He withdrew, rolling onto his back.

She focused on the cowbell hanging in the back window, its shadow crooked against the curtain.

"I'm sorry. I just started coming."

"You've never had to be sorry before." She zipped up her dress and moved back into the front seat.

"Jesus." He lay there a moment longer. The only sound was an occasional tired click from the engine.

He moved up front. "This was your idea."

"So I really forced you?"

"Yeah, I'd say in a way, you did."

She stared out at the ocean, a deep green except for the glow of the tide's foam.

"It just probably wasn't such a good idea," Kyle said, starting the van.

They didn't say anything more until he'd driven her home. As she was getting out of his van, she felt as if she was never going to see him again. He must have sensed this, still able to sense changes in her mood as easily as he could predict the best light for crabbing. "I love you, Vickie, you know that. Let's not drive each other crazy though, okay?"

She reached in through his window and cupped her hand over his on the steering wheel.

CHAPTER 19

THE MORNING AFTER the party, Vickie's father was having his coffee in the living room and her grandmother was sitting out in her Thunderbird. She'd heard Ruth up during the night, the sound of the candlesticks being shifted around on the sideboard, but Vickie didn't go downstairs.

"Where is everyone?"

"Gone to the beach," Blake said. "I think your uncle's a little hung over."

Although it wasn't so unusual for her father to

have stayed home, since he'd quickly grow restless sitting in the sun, Ruth always loved an excuse for an elaborate beach picnic, and Vickie was surprised she hadn't gone.

"I keep thinking she'll tire of that old car," Blake said. "But then what would she come home with, a Stanley Steamer?"

"What happened when you took her home last night?" Vickie asked.

"She wouldn't say a thing. Except that she was tired. Terribly tired." He lit a cigarette. "That party wasn't such a good idea after all."

They were quiet for a moment, and Vickie said, "So Catherine looked nice."

"Catherine?"

"Gail told us she bought the old Crest place. That she's from Chicago."

Blake took Piper into his lap. Rarely did he pick him up, never having been especially fond of cats. "Had a furniture repair business with her husband. They just got divorced."

"They must have had a good settlement for her to start a restaurant."

"We didn't get into the details."

"You spent most of the party with her."

He laughed. "Is that an accusation of some kind?"

"No . . . I just noticed, that's all."

He stroked Piper's tail.

"So are you going to see her again?"

"Well, she asked me over to see what she's doing to the old place. For some advice on fixtures."

Vickie nodded, looking out at Ruth. She was wearing Lydia's salmon wool sweater again.

"I thought this was what you wanted," Blake said.

"What I want? If it's what *you* want. . . . If you're ready. I didn't think you were, or at least that's what you said. . . ." She didn't know why she couldn't sound more convincing.

"Well, I guess I don't know that I am. Ready."

"You don't have to marry her, Dad."

He brushed Piper off his lap. "No. I guess I wasn't very good the first time around, anyway, was I?"

"Hasn't it ever occurred to you that maybe it was as much Mom? Don't you think at least *some* of it was her?"

He didn't say anything, feeling around the edges of his receding hairline. It occurred to Vickie then that whether he ever did remarry or not, he might always take just as much time with things like re-filling the salt and pepper shakers. He might always be feeling Lydia there.

"How are the Arnolds?" Blake asked, sounding relieved when Ruth came into the room.

"Why is it you always think I'm watching the

Arnolds? I was thinking. About how my family uses an extended visit as an excuse to go to the beach."

"You could have gone with them," Vickie said, annoyed with her for interrupting them.

"No, I couldn't have gone, Victoria—the least bit of sun now gives me brown spots." She sat on the edge of the velvet chair rather than sinking into it. "You know, I hope your sister understood. . . ."

"That you were tired?"

Ruth rubbed her bifocals on her sleeve.

"She's okay, Gramma."

Ruth nodded, getting up, and Vickie was alarmed by how stooped her grandmother seemed. "Where are you going?"

"To bed."

"To bed?"

Ruth hadn't gone back to bed after breakfast since that month she'd spent knitting after Lydia died.

"I just didn't sleep very well last night, dear," Ruth said as if she'd read Vickie's thoughts.

Vickie drove over to the hall to help her sister clean up, feeling a little guilty about not returning to the party last night. She knew Meryl would already be there, since their father didn't want to have to pay rent for another full day.

Meryl was collecting the plastic cups, which littered the floor, into a garbage bag, and her grass-stained sweatpants sagged around her hips. Her curls had fallen out, and she'd pulled back her hair with what looked like Alex's barrettes, a couple of blue plastic bows.

"It's disgusting, isn't it? All this waste," she said.

"You can recycle a lot of it," Vickie said.

"It's still disgusting." She handed Vickie the bag. "You finish; I'll clean off the tables."

Vickie moved around the hall doing as she was told, collecting cups stained with lipstick and cigarette ashes.

"You left in a hurry last night," Meryl said.

"Sorry."

"No matter. Needless to say, the party petered out rather quickly after that. It's just that I could have used your help cleaning up."

"I'm helping you now."

"My point is, you didn't have to run out like that."

"You just said it didn't matter."

"Oh, don't, Victoria."

"What?"

Meryl didn't say anything, crumpling the wrapping papers from the present table into tight balls and stuffing them into a plastic bag.

"It's not my leaving that upsets you anyway. It's that I left with Kyle."

Meryl stood there with the bag drooping from

one hand and her other hand on her hip. "What makes you so sure I wanted to give this party anyway?"

"Well, why'd you give it then?"

"Who else was going to?"

"Why'd we have to have a party in the first place? Maybe it was just too soon for us to be celebrating anything."

"But it's not too soon for Daddy to start dating?"

Vickie didn't answer.

"I just don't understand it, how Gramma could leave and not even say anything. She just *left*."

"She was tired . . . ," Vickie said vaguely.

"Oh, she wasn't tired."

Vickie watched her sister carefully folding a piece of wrapping as if it was worth saving, and she said, "She and Gail had a kind of falling-out."

"Gail? It was Gail?"

"It wasn't Gail—"

"You just said they had a fight."

"Gramma asked for it, Meryl. She kept baiting Gail about the dog."

"And you would stick up for her, even though she ruined your own grandmother's birthday party."

"Gramma didn't want this party in the first place, but you refused to see that."

"Of course, she wanted it. She just didn't need Gail ruining it."

"She didn't *want* it, Meryl."

For a moment, Meryl didn't say anything, her mouth so pinched her lips blanched. "You're so quick to criticize, but when do you lift a finger to make a difference? It wouldn't hurt for you to come up with the idea once in a while."

"You don't need to turn this around on me, just because you can't admit maybe you were wrong. That maybe your ideas aren't always the best ones."

"I'm not turning it around on you. But you talk about me being fair—it wouldn't hurt you to be a little more fair yourself. You'll never see that there might be another side to things."

"No one's ever seen *my* side."

"Mom just worried about you. She couldn't help worrying."

"What makes you think I'm talking about Mom?"

"Who else do you talk about these days?" Meryl sat down looking defeatedly around at the mess. "God, Vickie, don't you think she hurt me too? When she'd needle me with her little comments about why you were better at the piano was because my hands were too small?"

"And she'd tell me I wasn't any good at gymnastics because I was too big."

"The point is, she meant well. She didn't always say the right thing, but she meant well." Meryl looked at her nails that she'd polished for the party. "I made allowances for that."

She began chipping away at the polish, something Vickie hadn't seen her do since high school when she wore nail polish all the time. She'd sit like that during television commercials when she was too full of her own sense of privacy to share with Vickie much more than a bowl of popcorn.

"You think it was all my fault," Vickie said.

"What's your fault?"

"About me and Mom."

"I was talking in general, how you can be so judgmental sometimes."

"You were talking about Mom."

Meryl systematically chipped away at the polish, working her way up from the cuticles.

"You got along so well because you never faced up to her," Vickie said.

"And when did you face up to her? When you'd sneak around behind her back?"

Vickie knew she was talking about Kyle. "You did, too."

"That was different. She liked Glenn."

"And if she hadn't? Would you have dared to go out with him, anyway?"

"*Dared* to? I wouldn't have wanted to hurt her, if that's what you mean."

"You think I wanted to hurt her?"

"All I know is she tried, Vickie. She tried the only way she knew how."

"She never gave me a *chance*—"

"You never gave *her* a chance. She shouldn't have had to die like that, Vickie. She shouldn't have had to die thinking she didn't matter to you."

Vickie felt weak and sat down at a table. "She mattered to me. Of course, she mattered . . ."

"And what did you ever do to make her feel like that?" Meryl leaned on the table in front of Vickie. "How could she have *known?*"

Vickie stared up at her sister and saw every detail of her face, the tiny specks of brown in her green eyes, the dark patches of freckles around her nose, her eyebrows as faint as shadows. How unfamiliar she seemed; it had been so long since Vickie had really looked at her. Maybe not since the time she thought Meryl was dying—when Meryl had gone to the hospital with appendicitis and writhed so in pain. Vickie had memorized her face as they wheeled her away on a stretcher.

"I'm sorry," Meryl said, reaching toward Vickie.

Vickie pulled away from her. She left the hall, hearing her sister calling, "I'm *sorry!*"

CHAPTER 20

VICKIE WAS so used to seeking out Kyle, she didn't think twice about driving over to his place after running out on her sister. "Meryl and I had a fight."

Kyle was strapping his rowboat onto the top of his van to go spearfishing in Wheels Cove. "So what else is new?"

"She thinks Mom didn't know I loved her."

"Of course she knew—that's a given."

"Maybe not. Maybe not with the way we were."

"You let Meryl get to you too much, Vickie."

She was sitting on Kyle's front steps, and the gas pumps stared wistfully back at her from their rusted, worn faces.

"Anyway, good timing," he said, tossing an extra snorkel and wet suit into the van. Although he could manage the boat by himself, Vickie knew he appreciated having someone help slide it onto the Styrofoam tubes to roll down to the water.

Wheels Cove was named back in the late 1800s for a couple of carriages that had plunged off the cliff there in a storm—the wheels were now in the Sladebrook Museum. Kyle anchored near what he and Vickie called "The Old Man," an island of rocks resembling a wrinkled face. Beneath the water, the rocks formed a shallow cave where Kyle usually had the most luck spearing striped bass.

"Remember, a pace behind," he said, once they were in the water adjusting their masks and snorkels; he worried she'd swim ahead into the direct line of his gun.

The cave had always reminded Vickie of all the eerie spaces she'd ventured into as a kid: the boathouse, the old duck coops at the Engels farm, or just the hollow cavities of the bushes around their house. She'd found entering into that kind of void so liberating.

Panicked now by the greenish underwater glow,

she left Kyle. She quickly rose to the surface, longing for her mother so suddenly and so acutely the air seemed to have been knocked out of her. A longing not as though she had only to call for her mother in the next room when those handprints had seemed to move across her walls, but as though she might never see her alive again, as when they were once caught in a thunderstorm out biking together.

It had begun raining so hard that Vickie biked as fast as she could back to the house. Assuming her mother was following immediately behind her, she stood inside the front door waiting for her to appear around the corner of the street. Lightning flashed, and she imagined her mother being knocked off her bike. She even thought she heard her scream. It was the sound of Vickie's own scream.

Then her mother was there behind her, pulling her into the house so she could rub her dry with a towel. "I'm sorry, honey, I didn't see you. I thought you were ahead of me."

As if she were still waiting there in the doorway, Vickie would give anything for her mother to appear like that. She didn't think she could make it back to the boat, feeling as though she were merely treading water. So sure she couldn't make it, she considered giving herself up to the waves, half curious about whether drowning would be like drifting off to sleep.

Ripping off her snorkel and mask, she swam as hard as she could back to the boat.

"What's the matter with you?" Kyle called, swimming over to her. "I didn't know where the hell you'd gone."

She rested her forehead against the side of the boat.

"You okay?"

She nodded. "I lost the snorkel and mask."

"You *lost* them? Jesus."

She was too embarrassed to tell him she'd thought she was drowning; the water was so calm.

More concerned, he said, "Why don't you get in the boat? I want to go down one more time."

Vickie sat in the boat watching the orange tip of Kyle's snorkel bob in and out in the swell. Maybe he was right: her mother's awareness of Vickie's having loved her was a given. But that afternoon when she'd rubbed Vickie dry with a towel, she'd been so eager to make things right, and somewhere through the years that eagerness became muted. Especially somewhere around the time when Vickie became involved with Kyle.

"What were you thinking?" Lydia asked, confronting Vickie in the kitchen after Meryl had told her about Kyle.

"I didn't know what else to do," Vickie said. She'd just come home from seeing him.

"What else but *lie?*"

Vickie stood at the far end of the counter pressing her hand onto the Formica so that it was reflected in the toaster. "You wouldn't even try to get to know him—"

"This is a *crush*, Vickie," her mother said, waving her hands around in a sweeping arc. "A sixteen-year-old crush."

"Why can't you listen for once? Listen the way Kyle listens? Maybe you'd see I'm actually a lot wiser than you think."

"Wise? I know exactly how wise you are. You remind me every day, when I can't find a moment's peace." She was peeling carrots at the kitchen table and ran the blade back and forth across her thumb, wincing as if it hurt. "You're getting in over your head."

"See?" Vickie laughed, fighting back tears. "Every time I try to talk to you, you just talk back at me. Well, I'm already *in* over my head, Mom."

Lydia looked more dumbfounded than Vickie had ever seen her. "What are you saying?"

She didn't answer.

"Oh, Vickie . . ."

"It's all right, I went to a gynecologist . . . ," she began, never having intended to reveal so much.

Lydia stared into the colander.

"I'm just trying to tell you not to worry. That I'm taking care of myself."

220

She looked up at Vickie. "Is it me?"

"Is what you?"

"This. Why has it always been like this?"

Vickie swiveled her hand so that her fingers were distorted in the toaster.

Lydia took the carrots and colander over to the sink, asking, "Who took you? To the doctor?"

"I went by myself."

With her back to her, Lydia only nodded. Vickie wanted to tuck in the tag on her shirt but the gesture by then had become too awkward. Lydia didn't say anything more, seeming entirely resigned. As if she'd finally given up on her daughter.

Kyle speared a single striped bass, and while he cleaned it, Vickie rowed them out of the cove. He would have it filleted and sealed in a Ziploc bag to hide in his knapsack before they got back to the beach, since recreational fishing for striped bass was illegal in Lawton.

Usually she admired how swiftly he could slice off the flesh, but now she was sickened by the sight of the bluish entrails shrinking into themselves on the bottom of the boat. Blood ran down toward the stern, and she was reminded of Clara.

"You were everything to me," she said.

"What?"

"You were everything my mother tried to take away."

"And you didn't let her," Kyle said, studying the spine of the fish. "Do you wish you had?"

"I wish I didn't have to make a choice."

"She was the one who made you choose."

Vickie was suddenly angry. "She was looking out for me. For what she thought was best for me."

With rubberbands, he tied the spine and entrails around a stone to throw overboard. "You know, maybe Meryl says the things she says just out of envy."

"Envy?"

"Maybe she's always been a little jealous of you. Of the way you've been able to just get up and go."

"Since when do you know so much about my sister?"

He didn't say anything, diluting the blood with water from a coffee can so that he could more easily bail it out.

"You know, I compare everyone to you," she said.

"And what do you want me to say to that?" he snapped, and she was reminded of how impatiently he'd made love to her last night in the van.

The blood had turned the innocent pink of lemonade.

CHAPTER 21

GLENN CAME BY the hall with the kids to help Meryl fold up the tables and chairs, and Alex stayed outside to practice her cartwheels.

"I thought Vickie was going to help you," Glenn said.

"She was," Meryl said, sweeping the floor.

He laughed. "Can't you two get along for a minute?"

"I can't help it, Glenn. I get so tired of her feeling sorry for herself."

"Vickie? I wouldn't say she's exactly self-pitying."

"I didn't say self-pitying. It's just like she's owed something."

"Well, maybe she is."

"Don't, Glenn."

"I'm sorry. You just keep at her so. I don't re-member you being this . . . extreme somehow."

"Extreme?"

"You were accusing me of wanting to marry her instead, remember?"

Meryl was embarrassed by that now. "You made me angry."

"Lately, I'm always making you angry."

"So I have nothing to be angry about?"

"I didn't say you have nothing to be angry about." He took off his glasses to rub his eyes.

"You were the one to shut down the party."

"No, I think your grandmother did that all by herself."

"You didn't have to pack up the bar so that everyone would leave."

"It was getting out of hand, Meryl."

"And you just never wanted me to have that party to begin with," Meryl said, grabbing a streamer from Daryll as he was about to stuff it into his mouth.

"It's not . . ." He sighed. "You just didn't have to make it so elaborate, that's all."

She watched him for a moment as he began folding up the chairs. "Why do you need to make everything out to be me?"

"I'm not making—"

"First it's Alex, then it's Vickie."

"It's *not* you. None of this is you."

"And it's not you to shoot a dog."

Glenn grew quiet for a moment, then said, "I didn't know what I was doing, Meryl."

"You took the gun off the wall; you loaded it; you used it."

"And you've been making me crazy!"

She stared at him. "So that was me too?"

"Stop it, Meryl."

"I didn't pull the trigger, Glenn."

"Stop!"

Daryll was taking his shoes on and off, and Meryl wondered at his utter absorption. At how simply he was able to block them out.

"Why are you doing this?" Glenn took off his glasses again, this time to pinch away tears. "Why are you trying so hard to hurt us?"

Meryl refused to see him cry, and she started for the door.

"Jesus, Mel, don't," he said in a hoarse whisper. "Don't keep walking away."

She stopped when she saw Alex leaning against the doorjamb. Swinging her plastic beads, she seemed to have been standing there a long time.

Meryl couldn't look back at Glenn. "I just need . . . I'm just going for a short drive."

"A drive?"

One of Alex's socks had fallen down, and she allowed Meryl to pull it up. She was twisting her beads around and around her wrist, and Meryl couldn't remember her daughter looking so afraid. She took Alex's face in her hands to kiss her. "Honey, I'll be right back."

Meryl thought she'd walk for a while along the beach, but she ended up by driving over to Kyle's.

He was turning over the rowboat on the side of the house.

"She was here, wasn't she?" Meryl said, seeing the two wet suits spread out across the grass.

"I'd say you missed her by about three minutes," he said irritably.

"I'm sorry I wasn't thinking. . . ." She sat on the overturned boat, feeling foolish. She should have figured that Vickie would run to him.

"It's all right," he said, helping her up from the boat. "Come on in."

They sat in his garage he'd converted into a living room, sparsely furnished with yard-sale bargains such as the old sewing stand he used as a table and a frayed chair and couch draped with Indian bedspreads. It was as cluttered as her own house but with the most useless of things: a terrarium filled with decaying "Magic Rocks," a broken ceramic oil lamp decorated with flying pigs, and a dried blowfish hanging from the ceiling. To inflate it, Kyle had soaked the blowfish in the bathtub. He'd explained this to her after the first time they had sex and had nothing else to say to each other.

There had never been much they could say to each other. And when they had sex it was always in the dark, on those nights when she left her girlfriends early to meet Kyle. Sometimes before she had to pick up the kids from Gail's, she would come over, and Kyle would pull down all the shades in the bedroom. If they were on the couch, he wouldn't turn on a lamp. She didn't think he'd be able to make love to her in a light any brighter than the dull northern one falling in crooked squares through the row of small garage-door windows.

"What did she say?" Meryl asked.

"Vickie?"

"We had a fight."

"That's what she said."

"Anything else?"

"You really want to talk about her?"

They'd never been able to talk about her. But tracing that fine angle of his cheekbone, she asked, "What would you do if we both showed up here at the same time?"

"I don't like to think about that." He removed her hand and gently placed it on her own knee. "And

I don't think we should probably be doing this anymore."

"I know . . . ," she said, not prepared for how her voice broke.

"You okay?"

"You still love her."

"You knew that."

She did know that. She knew it when she'd seen them together across the parking lot. She knew it by how differently he treated her than Vickie. They never could have been at ease enough to make something together like the cow kite dangling from the garage door handle that she remembered from the *Gazette*. She'd try to show some interest in his psychology books by occasionally browsing through one from his shelf, but he'd take it from her, saying, "Just more scientific jargon."

She wondered why she'd tried so hard to show interest in something that didn't interest her anyway. She supposed it was to please him, although she didn't know why she cared about pleasing him, either. But from the time she first ran into him at her friend's wedding reception, she had made a point of running into him again and again, taking Daryll to the annual Lawton Easter egg hunt and the spring fair, events she knew Kyle probably would be covering for the newspaper.

By then, she hadn't thought her stopping by his

place unexpectedly would be so unforeseen. She hadn't thought that she would actually have to ask him to make love to her.

He'd been working out back and he didn't answer, scanning his recently tilled yard. She'd finally gone over to him, tentatively running her hands along his bare arms. "Please . . ."

She wasn't in love with him now any more than she had been then, when she'd had to plead with him in a way that had been humiliating but somehow inevitable. What mattered was that being with Kyle freed the ache between her ribs; it was lifted away as easily as an old leaf. She could feel as she could before her fear of heights, when she'd even been able to cross the Ridge, the most narrow strip of the stone embankment above the railroad tracks just past the willow trees. Although she had never played around the tracks as a child, in high school she and Glenn would cross the Ridge to reach a secluded clearing where they could make love. She remembered being able to look down, to feel the push and pull of the wind without being afraid of falling.

Kyle shifted on the couch. "Listen, Vickie doesn't ever have to know about any of this. She can't."

Meryl got up abruptly. He seemed to have forgotten that she, too, had something at stake. "Neither can Glenn."

She left, knowing she would not be coming there again. But she sensed things weren't quite over; backing out of his driveway, she imagined her mother emerging from the cattails that lined his yard, having tried to camouflage herself among their tall reeds.

CHAPTER 22

SHE HASN'T BEEN gone all that long. It takes that long just to bike over here," Vickie said, annoyed that Meryl had insisted she drive around with her to look for Alex. Vickie had come home from Kyle's exhausted and had fallen asleep on the couch.

"Well, she's not here, is she? And she's not at Gail's."

Vickie put her feet up on Meryl's dashboard.

"I can't help it, I have this feeling."

"You're always having a 'feeling.' Like when

you think a tornado three states over is going to stop over your own house."

"Look, she heard me and Glenn kind of arguing over at the hall. . . . All I know is, when we got home she took off on her bike and hasn't come back."

"Don't tell me you think she ran away."

Meryl didn't say anything.

"You do."

"Who knows what goes on in her head these days? She's rarely around."

"Does Glenn think she ran away?"

"I don't know what he thinks. So where should we look first?"

"How should I know?"

"You do know—she talks to you."

"She doesn't talk to me, Meryl."

"Please, Vickie."

Vickie glanced back at her grandmother's house as they turned out of the driveway. She noticed the black shutters were peeling and this made her suddenly very sad. "Try the old boathouse on Bell Lake."

"There's a boathouse there?"

"Take Whitehill Street and there's a dirt road off into the woods."

They turned onto Whitehill, and Vickie remembered biking past the fields there and frightening flocks of geese so that they took flight.

"Sorry about before," Meryl said.

"Don't placate me, Meryl."

"I'm not placating you."

"You're not sorry either."

"You want to make this into something, don't you?"

"It already is something." The car smelled of wet diapers and Vickie rolled down her window. "You were probably right anyway."

"Oh, I don't know that I was right. . . . God, I don't even know if she knew *I* loved her."

"You'll say anything to keep the peace, won't you?"

"Give me a break, Vickie."

Vickie leaned her head out the window inhaling the fragrance of lilac. "How could she *not* know?"

Meryl didn't answer, and Vickie could see that something was deeply troubling her by the way she chewed the inside of her mouth.

"You were so *there* for her, Mel."

"And how much do you think she noticed?"

Vickie sat up, taking her feet down from the dashboard. "You two were always talking—"

"Sure, we talked. I know we *talked*. But she'd be so busy trying to get her hair right, she'd hardly notice me."

"What?"

"For those dances. You know, I used to watch

her. . . ." Meryl began, and Vickie was reminded of how embarrassed she herself had felt alluding to her old music recital.

"Anyway, she'd look at me in the mirror but didn't seem to see me. Like when we'd be talking about you—she was just so busy trying to get things right."

Vickie was reminded of what Kyle had said about Meryl being jealous. "She got things right with you."

Meryl whipped her head around, angry enough for red spots to break out on her face like they could on Ruth's.

"You're the one she was proud of," Vickie said.

"Why? Because I never caused a commotion?"

Vickie noticed something then that she hadn't when Meryl was leaning over her at the hall—creases around Meryl's eyes and at the corners of her mouth. Her sister was actually beginning to show signs of age.

"All I'm saying is, I didn't necessarily know any better than you did what exactly was going on with Mom all the time," Meryl said. "Only . . . I don't know. You couldn't always know what was going through her mind. I mean, maybe that was it—in the end, she just felt she couldn't get anything right."

Meryl now seemed to be the one leaning toward the idea of suicide, and for the first time it was Vickie who didn't want to be talking about it.

"Turn here," Vickie said, glad when they came to the dirt road.

They had to walk most of the way to the lake, since they were able to park only halfway down the road. "How did you ever find this place?" Meryl asked, whacking a path through the bittersweet.

"It wasn't so overgrown back then."

Once they were at the house, Vickie peered through an opening where the boards nailed across the broken window had rotted off. In one corner was a kind of broom she imagined Alex had made, out of ferns tied to the end of a branch. When Vickie had pretended it was her own house, she'd used birch bark for a dust pan.

"Damn her. Where is she?" Meryl kicked the side of the house. "Why is she doing this to me?"

"She's not doing anything to you."

"She's doing *this* to me!" Meryl yelled, tossing a rock into the lake with a force Vickie didn't know she had.

"She's okay, Mel," Vickie said, although she was beginning to worry a little herself. "There are a couple of other places we can check. Maybe she's even home by now."

By dusk, Alex was still missing, and Glenn went out to search with the police. Meryl cupped her face against the window as if she could see farther than the edge of their bushes. Reflected in the window, the lamp on the opposite wall hung above her head like a cold winter sun, and Vickie couldn't remember her sister ever looking so lonely.

Vickie didn't want to leave her, but Meryl asked if she'd go back out since she had to put Daryll to bed.

"I'm spending the night, though," Vickie said.

Meryl only nodded without moving from the window.

Vickie drove down every back road she could remember exploring on her bike and, having no luck, stopped home for a change of clothes. Uncle Warren and Phillip themselves had just returned from driving around, and her father had gone out.

"She's been kidnapped," Ruth announced, pacing behind the velvet chair. "It's epidemic in all the supermarkets. Parents turn their backs for an instant and their children are snatched from their carts."

"And in which tabloid did you see that headline?" Vickie asked, in no mood for her grandmother's declarations.

"Maybe she has run away," Phillip said. Shawna had taken Gordon up to bed, and Phillip was folding a bib on his knee as Vickie had seen him fold laundry, meticulously smoothing out the wrinkles. "You can never really know what's going on in those complex little brains of theirs."

"She hasn't been kidnapped; she hasn't run

away," Vickie said, feeling suddenly exhausted. "She biked too far this time, that's all."

"Well, we might as well try to get at least some sleep," Uncle Warren said, tossing one of the Christmas balls from the mantel back and forth between his hands. Despite his sunburn from the beach, he still looked hung over.

"Sleep? How can you think of sleep?" Ruth said, kneading the back of the chair. "We should all be out there, every one of us."

"The police are looking, Mother," Uncle Warren said.

"And I'm going out myself."

Uncle Warren laughed. "In what? That old car of yours?"

Vickie expected her grandmother to look as embarrassed as she would whenever he brought up the subject of the car.

She ignored Uncle Warren as she lifted the lamp from the piano. She unscrewed its cylindrical bottom, and a set of keys fell out.

"So that's where," Vickie said.

"Anyone care to join me?"

"You're being childish, Mother," Uncle Warren said.

Ruth started toward him, and Vickie thought she might slap him again. But she headed into the hall, and the china bowl on the chest rattled as she slammed the front door.

"She's not really going to drive, is she?" Phillip asked. He had been there the time she ran over the rock at the end of the driveway.

"She can't," Vickie said. "That battery must be long since dead."

The engine turned over, and they all went out on the front steps.

"What's going on?" Shawna asked, elbowing her way through them.

The engine stalled and Ruth tried again.

"My God," Shawna exclaimed.

"She'll never get it going . . . ," Vickie said, less certain now.

Ruth did get the engine going and the car jolted forward. It stalled again but continued rolling anyway, picking up speed down the hill. The silver fins gleamed brilliantly in the streetlight.

"What the hell . . . ?" Uncle Warren ran down the hill.

This time, Ruth missed actually running over the rock but one tire sideswiped it so that the car lurched onto the lawn and slammed into the spruce tree.

Uncle Warren opened the car door. "Mother . . . ?"

Ruth sat there looking dazed.

"You all right, Gramma?" Vickie asked.

Uncle Warren helped her out of the car.

"Did she hit her head?" Shawna asked, her voice shaking. "Did you hit your head, Gramma?"

Snapping to, Ruth said irritably, "No, I didn't hit my head." She peered around the front of the car. "Oh, no." The left headlight had shattered against the tree.

"Didn't you brake?" Vickie asked.

"Of course, I braked. I pressed it to the floor."

"Then the brakes don't *work,* Gramma," Vickie said.

"Why else do you think I got such a good price on it?"

"You knew the brakes were bad, and you bought the car anyway?" Vickie asked.

"I knew I wasn't going to be driving it."

"You just *were* driving it—"

"You could have been hurt, Gramma," Shawna said, taking off her sweater to drape around Ruth's shoulders as if she looked cold.

Pulling the sweater around her, Ruth gathered up the shards from the headlight. She held them out under the streetlamp as if she were considering gluing them together.

"I should go up to the house," Phillip said, hovering behind them like a bystander, as he had hovered the first time Ruth's car got stuck at the end of the driveway. "I don't know if we can hear Gordon from here."

They all watched Phillip walk up to the house as if they weren't going to be seeing him for a long while.

"So are you satisfied, Mother?" Uncle Warren asked.

"You think this was my intention?"

"You said yourself you knew the brakes were bad."

"Somebody had to *do* something."

He laughed. "And you certainly did."

Ruth let the shards fall as if they were sunflower seeds she might be scattering around her birdbath for her favorites, the juncos. "Oh, dear."

"Mother, . . . I'm sorry." Uncle Warren said, putting his arm around her.

Ruth shook him off. "You're hardly sorry."

"Can't you give in, just a little?"

"Then why weren't you there?"

Uncle Warren scratched behind his ear so that it stuck out farther.

"Why weren't you, Warren? She would have wanted you, she would have wanted you there."

Uncle Warren pulled at the seams of his pants, and he looked so much like a young boy then. A young awkward boy.

"Let him be," Vickie said.

"Let him be?" Ruth echoed confusedly.

Uncle Warren rested his hand flat against the hood of the Thunderbird as if he were trying to feel for something other than its rusted surface.

"I'm going to get going back to Meryl's," Vickie said.

"My poor child. Where is she? Where *is* she?" Ruth cried out, and for a moment Vickie thought it was Lydia her grandmother was calling out for.

CHAPTER 23

ERYL WATCHED as her son dreamed, the way his mouth twitched slightly and his eyes coursed back and forth beneath his lids. She trailed her fingers lightly down his stomach as she used to like trailing her fingers down Alex's when she was sleeping. She couldn't remember now the last time she'd been able to touch her daughter, not without her pulling away. Except for yesterday, when Alex had allowed her to pull up her sock.

But Meryl had gotten into her car. She'd driven

over to Kyle's. Nausea rose in her throat as if she were teetering precariously far above Daryll's crib.

Meryl went back into the kitchen, where Glenn was pouring a jar of sauce into a pot of spaghetti. "I made enough for Vickie when she gets back," he said, sitting at the table.

Meryl swallowed hard to squelch that nausea as she stared at the tangle of strands he piled onto her plate.

"You have to eat, Mel."

"I'm not hungry."

"We won't get through this if you don't keep your strength up."

He twirled his spaghetti around and around his fork, seeming to enjoy it as much as at any other meal, and she said, "How can you?"

"How can I what?"

"Eat? How can you eat?"

He laughed, raising his hands in surrender. "Well, forgive me—I confess, I'm actually hungry. Hungry and tired. And when I go back out to look for our daughter, I'd prefer not falling asleep behind the wheel."

Meryl cupped her hands against the window trying to see out through the reflections of the room, and the worst of all possibilities came to mind—that something terrible was happening to Alex right now. Right at this moment. "I'm going out."

"Vickie's looking, Mel, and I'm going out too.

And if anyone can find her, it will be the police. They at least have searchlights."

"They don't know our daughter."

"Neither do you."

She leaned back against the window to consider him.

"You don't know any more than I do where she'd go, Mel. If we did, maybe we would have found her by now."

"I can't sit here, Glenn. I can't just *sit* here."

"Try to keep your head, okay?"

"I'm not losing my head. I just can't stand her being out there."

"You will lose your head if you don't eat something," he said, pointing to her plate.

She watched him scrape up the last of his sauce. "Can't you worry about your daughter for once?"

"You actually think I'm not worried?"

"You never thought anything could happen. You insisted on giving her free rein on that goddamn bike."

"That has nothing to do with it."

"It has everything to do with it."

"What did you want, for us to take her bike away?"

"We could have set limits."

"And how would we know she'd stick to those limits unless we're breathing down her neck every hour of the day? She has a mind of her own, Meryl."

"She's *ten years old*. Why can't you remember that, that she's a child? She's ten years old?"

He put on his jacket. "You know, it's not her disappearing on her bike that upsets you anyway. It's that she's staking out her own territory, and that doesn't happen always to include you."

He put on his cap and she watched him adjust the visor as if he were merely going over to the spec house.

"Am I that selfish, Glenn?"

"You won't let her be herself is what it is, like with Vickie."

"Vickie? We have to talk about Vickie again?"

"I can't help it, Meryl. You're doing to Alex what your mother did to Vickie—she wouldn't let her be herself, either, and neither will you."

As he was leaving, she asked, "And what do you do except this, take the easy way out?"

"Now my going out to look for her is the easy way out?"

"You're really good at this, lecturing me on how I'm doing everything wrong in bringing up my own daughter, but how do you really contribute, Glenn?"

"How do I contribute? I pay the bills for that damn private school, that's how I contribute."

"You know that's not what I mean. And, anyway, you know Ruth—"

"Don't start, Meryl."

"Well, you could, Glenn. You could give up a

little of your stubborn pride for the sake of your children's education."

"Education for what? Proper table manners?"

Meryl felt her chest growing tight. "What I *meant* was, how do you ever really put yourself on the line for her?"

Glenn took the truck's keys from the hook by the door, and Meryl thought he would just leave.

"How do *I* put myself on the line?" he said, turning around to face her. "And what about you? Where have you been? Who's the one out fucking around!"

The blood drained from Meryl's face, and her skin grew clammy.

"If you weren't so preoccupied with your own little escapade, maybe we wouldn't be going through this."

Her tongue felt too dry and thick to speak.

"You really think I'd never find out? That I'd never know?" Glenn squinted as if he couldn't stand the sight of her. "Don't you think *she* knows?"

Meryl supported herself by leaning back against the refrigerator.

"I followed you after you drove off from the hall."

Revived a little by the cold surface of the freezer's door, she was able to ask, "With the kids?"

"They didn't see your car there—only if they'd been looking for it." Sounding more tired now than angry, he said, "Alex doesn't *actually* know. I just think she knows this hasn't been us. How could she not know, Mel?"

A car pulled into the driveway and Meryl ran to the window, hoping it was the police.

"It's Vickie," Meryl said. She looked back at Glenn.

"And what if I did tell her?" he asked.

Vickie came in, asking, "Any word?"

Meryl's entire body went rigid.

Neither answered.

"I guess that means no," Vickie said.

"There's some spaghetti there," Glenn said, walking past her.

After he'd left, Vickie said, "Ruth rammed her T-bird into that spruce tree."

Meryl supposed she should be alarmed. She couldn't feel anything except for a slight tingling in her hands and feet, all that was left of any sensation.

Daryll grinned at himself reflected in one of the mirrors propped against the house. He held his arms outstretched, pretending to fly.

"What bird are you?" Meryl asked, standing behind him.

"A crow."

Meryl held her own arms outstretched. "A crow? A big black crow?"

The mirror gave way and they were buoyed above it on a breeze. They rose higher and higher, and she had to strain to see their reflections. Soon they disappeared entirely against a murky gray sky, but she wasn't afraid of falling. She woke to a stiff neck with her head on the kitchen table.

Although it was only six-thirty in the morning, she felt as groggy as if she'd been sleeping for hours. It was just a couple of hours ago when she and Vickie had come in from their shifts looking for Alex, when the police had last checked in, and Glenn had gone out again. Vickie hadn't moved from the couch, and Meryl wondered whether her sister would always be able to sleep so soundly. Whether she would ever have to know anything the least bit like this, the possibility of having lost a part of herself.

Last night, Meryl was sure Glenn would have told Vickie about Kyle if only out of revenge, but even then his consideration of Vickie seemed to have gotten the better of him. Once Meryl no longer had been able to hear his truck, the sensation gradually returned in her arms and legs and she'd been able to make a pot of coffee.

"So Ruth's okay?" Meryl had asked, staring into the freezer as if searching for more than the bag of coffee beans.

"She's fine, although the car's not, with a dented

fender and broken headlight. Then she started in on Uncle Warren for not being at the funeral."

"And how'd that come up?"

"I don't know. It's like everything else these days, I guess," Vickie said, peering into the practically full pot of spaghetti. "Did you eat any yourself?"

"Maybe later. You want coffee?"

"You'd feel better if you had something besides caffeine burning a hole in your stomach."

"I'm asking if you want coffee."

"A cup, I'll have a cup."

Meryl measured out the beans and was grateful for the loud whir of the grinder.

When she turned the grinder off, Vickie said, "Alex is all right, Mel."

"Sure. She's been gone eight hours. She's fine."

"You have to keep some perspective—"

"*You* keep perspective. After all, that's your privilege, isn't it?"

"My privilege?"

"It's not *your* daughter that's missing."

Vickie twirled her spaghetti around and around her fork, and Meryl was reminded of how Glenn had seemed so to enjoy his own meal.

"All I'm trying to say is, this isn't your fault," Vickie said.

"I didn't say it was."

"You were the one who said she ran away."

"*You* said that."

"But isn't that what you're thinking, the way you insist on taking responsibility for everything? Some things are maybe out of your hands, Mel, but you have such a hard time accepting that."

Meryl wasn't used to her sister sounding so rational and patient. "And you don't take responsibility for *anything*."

Vickie frowned. "Right."

"Well, you don't, Vickie. Look at the choices you keep making."

"Why does everything come back to me and my life? This isn't about me, it's about Alex."

Meryl didn't say anything.

"They're just not your choices, Mel."

"My choices?" Meryl slammed down Vickie's cup in front of her. "And what are my choices?"

Vickie looked at her so curiously, Meryl said, "Maybe I just get tired of having to look out for you, that's all."

"You don't have to look out for me. No one ever asked you to look out for me."

"No? Then why don't you start taking a little responsibility for things?"

"Why don't you let me?"

"Let you?" Meryl laughed.

"You don't know how *not* to look out for me,

Meryl. Because you don't know how to do anything else."

Meryl stared into the sink. She stared at the bits of egg from that morning's breakfast still in the drain.

"I didn't mean—"

"I know what you meant."

Meryl had always known. She knew there were things Vickie thought she could never comprehend. Once Meryl had asked Vickie what she saw in Kyle, and Vickie had answered with a shrug from where she lay reading on her bed, "Nothing you can see."

The fact was, Meryl hadn't been able to see what her sister saw in Kyle. At least not what she could see in him now, and watching Vickie sleep, for a moment she wished Glenn had actually told her.

She heard the back door open.

It was Alex.

"God." Meryl could only look at her, at how she was simply there.

"Honey? You okay? Are you okay?"

Alex didn't answer, but she allowed Meryl to examine her face and neck, to feel for bumps or cuts on her scalp. Her nails were caked with dirt. She gripped her pink box tightly as if someone might steal it.

Vickie sat up on the couch blinking sleepily. "Alex?"

"Where were you? Did the police bring you?" Meryl asked, even though if the police had brought her, she wouldn't have appeared alone at the back door.

Alex wouldn't answer her.

"Where were you, Alex? Where's your bike?" Meryl lifted her face so that Alex would have to look at her. "Where *were* you?"

"Nowhere."

"Don't tell me that. Don't tell me nowhere."

Alex tried to pull away.

"Not until you tell me."

Alex tugged at Meryl's hands.

"*Tell* me, Alex. Don't you have any idea what we've been going through?"

"Nowhere! I wasn't anywhere!" Alex kicked Meryl in her shin so that Meryl stumbled, catching herself on the edge of the table.

"You killed her!" Alex yelled. "You killed Clara!" She ran to her room.

Meryl sat at the table, staring at the floor. She wondered at how evenly grouted the tiles were. At how anything could be so remarkably uniform.

"Maybe she *wasn't* anywhere," Vickie said.

Meryl forced herself to look over at her sister, who'd gotten up from the couch. She was changing into a clean T-shirt, and for a moment Meryl glimpsed her bare chest, so broad and yet small-breasted, she wondered how Kyle had ever been attracted to her.

"Maybe she was right here all the time, hiding somewhere," Vickie said. "Maybe she just wanted to give you a scare."

"Is that what you think I deserve, a scare?"

"No, I don't think you deserve a scare, Mel. I just hope you're not taking it to heart, what she said."

"Maybe I did kill Clara."

"Of course, you didn't—"

"Oh, shut up, Vickie."

Vickie only nodded, and Meryl could no longer bear her sister's quiet patience. "You just have no right, do you understand? You have no *right*. You complain about Uncle Warren, but you were on the first flight out. And then you don't come home for how many months and think you can piece it all together."

Putting on her jacket, Vickie said, "You know, you just wish you could blame all this on me like you blame me for Mom."

"Oh, give it up, Vickie."

"It's true, Meryl; you know it is."

"Stop pretending to have everything figured out, will you? You don't have everything figured out. Because you don't know a thing. You don't know anything about what's been going on. You don't even know about Kyle."

"Kyle? And what would you know about Kyle?"

Meryl couldn't help being amused by her sister's complete lack of suspicion. "You couldn't even guess, could you?"

"Guess what?"

"That it's me."

Vickie slipped her hands into her jacket pockets and Meryl could see how they were balled there.

"What's you?" Vickie asked.

"Glenn knows."

"Glenn knows what?"

"That it's *me,* Victoria," Meryl said, struck by the utter absurdity of it all. "That I've been having an affair." She laughed. "I've been having an affair with my sister's old boyfriend." She couldn't help laughing.

Vickie backed away from her, toward the door. "You've lost it."

"It is hard to believe, isn't it?"

"Why are you doing this?"

"Ask him."

Vickie left, closing the door quietly.

"Ask him! Ask Kyle!"

CHAPTER 24

KYLE'S FRONT DOOR was open and Vickie went in and sat on the bench opposite his darkroom. She knew he was in there because she could hear his radio, the small old one he kept on a shelf beside the miniature plastic gum ball machine that had been empty for as long as she'd known him. The only reason he was up so early must have been because he was behind in print jobs.

When he came out, he stopped short. "Well,

hello," he said, sounding pleased but surprised. "You been here long?"

"Not long," she said hoarsely, wondering now why she was there, why she should be listening to Meryl. She cleared her throat. "Alex was missing. She was gone all night."

"All *night?*"

"She's okay. She came back this morning."

"Where was she?"

"She won't say."

"But she's okay?"

"She seems to be."

"Jesus." He went over to the light box he kept on an old washstand to examine a pile of contact sheets. "That must have given Meryl and Glenn a few white hairs."

Vickie got up so that she could watch him, the way his mouth curled as he squinted through the loupe.

"I had to take five rolls of this guy, just for a damn book jacket," Kyle said. "But he insisted on having it with his parrot, and every time I was about to take a shot, the parrot would move to the other shoulder."

"I need to know who you're seeing."

He looked at her for a moment, then back at the contact sheets.

"Who is it, Kyle?"

"Please, Vickie."

"Who *is* it?"

"Don't. Let's not, all right?"

By the way he was hurriedly shifting the loupe around the sheet, she could tell he was trying to disguise how his fingers shook.

"You bastard." She swept the contact sheets off the light box. "You fucking bastard."

"Vickie . . . ," he said, moving toward her, and she shoved him away. She shoved him again, and he grabbed her arms. His firm hold made her want to hit him all the more, and she struggled against him until they fell. She punched him in the chest, and he pushed her off him so that she banged her head against the wall.

She lay there staring at the ceiling, waiting for the sharp pain in the back of her head to subside.

"Oh, Vickie . . ." He crawled over to her.

She pulled herself up so that she could lean against the wall.

"I'm sorry."

She started to cry.

"I didn't plan it, Vickie."

She cried like she used to when she'd hide in the recesses around the cellar windows hoping no one would find her. Hoping her mother and Meryl and everyone else would leave her alone.

"She was just . . . there, Vickie. She put herself there."

"She never liked you. . . . She never *liked* you."

"And I think she still doesn't like me. But I don't know how much that mattered—it was something she seemed to need."

"*Need?*"

"She asked herself over here, Vickie. She finally just asked herself over. . . ."

Vickie couldn't think. None of this was making any sense. "Why my sister? Why did it have to be my *sister?*"

"I don't know."

"You didn't have to give in. Why'd you give in?"

"I didn't think it out, Vickie."

"You should have. You should have *thought it out*. Why? Why didn't you think it out?"

He didn't answer.

"*Why?*"

He began gathering up the contact sheets, and his silence infuriated her. "Damn it, Kyle!"

"What?" he yelled, now tossing the sheets. "What is it you want to hear? Maybe she was just the closest I could get to you, Vickie, maybe that's why."

She looked at him, not knowing how to feel.

"You don't want us to be together, but you don't want me to see anyone either. And that doesn't mean only your sister." He started toward the back door. "You're just putting on a show, anyway, Vickie. A big show about leading your own life. But that's all it is, a show."

He went outside, and in a moment she could hear him hammering together the frames for his tiered garden beds.

She stared at the contact sheets scattered around her and thought briefly about picking them up for him. She didn't. She left, feeling as though she were wading through a stagnant pond.

CHAPTER 25

*A*LEX KNELT by her bed unpacking her makeup box across her spread, and Meryl longed to get her into the tub, to rid her of wherever she'd been.

Daryll tried to swipe her bones off the spread.

"Leave me alone! Tell him to leave me alone!" Alex yelled.

Meryl balled a pair of Alex's socks, one of Daryll's favorite distractions, to roll across the room. She sat on the floor beside Alex. "Honey, the police are going to have to fill out a report. They'll want to know where you've been."

Alex tried to hook her pinky through the coiled tail of the seahorse.

"They'll need to know if anything happened to you. If anything bad happened."

"Nothing happened," she mumbled.

"Honest?"

She nodded.

"So no one hurt you? No one did anything to you?"

"No . . . ," Alex said, sounding disappointed, and Meryl believed her.

Feeling suddenly depleted, Meryl lay on her daughter's bed, and together they pushed around the bones as if they were doing a puzzle. Alex moved her hand near her mother's, and Meryl knew how much her daughter yearned now to be comforted. Meryl fought giving in as fiercely as if she were trying not to look down from a cliff. She could not give in until she knew where Alex had been.

"Maybe I'll go take a bath . . . ," Alex said, playing with her mother's fingers, twisting Meryl's wedding ring.

It was the first time Meryl could remember Alex volunteering to take a bath. "Well, not until we talk to the police, honey."

"I don't want to talk to them."

"The police are one people you can't say no to. Unless you talk to me first."

Alex began to pack up her bones.

"If you tell me, maybe you won't have to talk to them at all."

"I was in the barn."

"The barn?" Meryl sat up on the edge of the bed. "You were in the barn all this time?"

Alex nodded.

"That was the first place the police checked. Where? Where in the barn?"

"The rafters . . ."

"In the rafters? How'd you get into the rafters?"

"I climbed," she said simply.

"Alex, You could have fallen—"

"I wasn't there the whole time, I didn't *sleep* there. . . . I slept under Daddy's worktable."

Meryl's heart broke at the image of her daughter curled up beneath that old tin table. "Why? Why all this?"

Alex shrugged, snapping shut her box. She flipped the handle back and forth. Back and forth.

Meryl untangled Alex's hair from beneath her collar. "You are, aren't you? You're so afraid."

Alex looked at her mother in the same way that she had when Meryl was leaving the hall to drive over to Kyle's. "I'm *not* afraid . . . ," she said, her voice trailing off into tears. Meryl stroked her hair, and leaning her head on her mother's knee, Alex seemed to fall into a trance, watching Daryll roll the balled socks across the room.

Her eyes finally closed, and Meryl took off her shoes. She couldn't imagine that Alex had been able to sleep at all out there in the pitch dark. At night, they had to leave the bathroom light on for her.

"Well, this has been something," Glenn said wearily, after he'd come home and they'd filled out a police report. Alex was still sleeping. "Did she talk to you?"

"Kind of." Meryl lifted Daryll from his chair, having finally gotten around to giving him breakfast. "I think she's not feeling very . . . safe."

"Safe?"

"I guess she does know. In her own way."

Glenn opened a beer even though it was only ten in the morning.

"I'm surprised you didn't say anything," Meryl said. "Once you knew."

He sat on the couch, pushing aside a couple of magazines as if to see the photographs better beneath the glass. "I was worried. About what it would do to us."

Meryl took a long moment to sponge off the tray on Daryll's high chair.

"Why *Kyle?*"

"I don't really know," Meryl said. "I kept running into him."

"You kept running into him?"

She looked out the window at the chickens pecking at some cabbage leaves she'd tossed a couple of days ago. Before all this. "Anyway, it's over. We called it off."

"Did you, now," Glenn said evenly.

"I can't explain it, Glenn. Honest to God."

"Honest to God?"

"It was a *mistake*. I'm telling you I know it was a mistake."

"And that's supposed to make everything okay?"

"Well, what is it? You want to leave? You want me to beg you not to leave me?"

"You think it's that simple? I'd just get up and walk out on the kids?"

Daryll sat astride his favorite toy, the vacuum, and as he rode it across the floor, the wheels knocked noisily against the tiles.

"The thing is, you're not in love with him anyway," Glenn said.

"You're so sure of that?"

He laughed. "Are you? Are you actually in love with Kyle?"

She didn't answer him; of course she wasn't.

"If you were, maybe I'd be able to figure all this out. But I can't figure it out. I can't figure *you* out."

"And I can't figure you out, either, Glenn."

"Me? Have I been the one out fooling around?"

"That wasn't you, Glenn, shooting that dog."

"Don't try bringing that into this, Meryl."

"You *wouldn't,* Glenn. You wouldn't shoot a dog. I can't believe you even remembered where we kept the bullets."

"I had every right to shoot it, Meryl. If I'd known it was Gail's—"

"I'm not talking about your rights. I'm talking about what you would and wouldn't do."

Glenn got up and fidgeted with the knobs and faucets on the bookshelf.

"I just don't think you can explain that away . . . ," Meryl said.

"Don't talk to me about explaining things away!" Glenn yelled, starting toward her.

This time, Meryl didn't back up against the refrigerator. He was the one to move away from her.

He sat at the table. "Christ, what is this?"

She didn't know. She didn't know what this was. She'd never been here before. It was an even stranger place than where she'd been with Kyle. Daryll grinned at her, and she realized her face must be expressionless as he disconsolately reached down to spin one of the wheels.

"Well . . . what? Are you thinking of leaving *me?*" Glenn asked.

"Like you said, it's not that simple."

He looked at her expectantly, and she was surprised herself that she couldn't tell him no.

CHAPTER 26

VICKIE LAY AWAKE unable to believe she was actually missing Kyle. Missing him as she could when trying to fall asleep after having sex in someone else's bed, when she'd study the unfamiliar outline of a chair whose fabric she couldn't recall or the jagged horizon of indistinguishable objects strewn across a bureau. When she couldn't help feeling displaced, as if deposited from another planet.

She heard the kettle being turned off as it began to whistle, and she went downstairs.

"I thought you were Gramma," she said, embarrassed; she couldn't ever remember seeing Uncle Warren in his pajamas before.

Tightening his bathrobe belt as if he was embarrassed himself, he asked, "She's still up nights?"

"Usually looking for something. The other night it was a stone from her pin."

He leaned back against the stove, clutching his mug against his chest so that he seemed oddly like a child grappling with too big an object. "It's been rather a confusing few days, hasn't it?"

"At least Alex is all right," Vickie said, trying to think of anything to say. She didn't remember there ever having been just the two of them. She hoped he'd forgotten telling her the story about the watch.

"She's quite a little character, isn't she, hiding in the barn all night?"

"I think that probably has to do with something more than character."

"No, I guess you don't worry your parents sick for no good reason. And it always does come back to the parents, doesn't it? A least she's not playing water witch down in the basement." He pointed to the kettle. "Should be still hot."

Wondering why she didn't go back to bed, Vickie poured herself a cup of chamomile, saying, "Gramma's remedy."

"Your mother used to get up too and I'd hear them playing cards."

"Double solitaire."

"Some things don't change, do they? Especially around here. I can't even get your grandmother to get that fixed," he said, shaking his head at the crack above the stove that leaked after most rainstorms. "She'd rather wait for the entire wall to cave in."

"Well, that's your mother."

He looked at her.

"She's just being Gramma. Like with buying that car."

He nodded thoughtfully, and tightening his belt again, said, "You know . . . I really couldn't get a flight."

Vickie sat on the stool in the far corner of the kitchen. "And if you could have?"

He hugged his mug against his chest so that he seemed like a child again, and Vickie could imagine his father pressing the watch into his hand. She could imagine him scratching behind one ear, trying to make sense out of being told that he was now the one to take care of the family.

"You couldn't have saved her," she said.

Uncle Warren flinched.

Not prepared for how disarmed he seemed, she said, "I mean, no one could. . . ."

"No," he said, now noticing how he'd been clutching his mug. He took it by its handle. "And

I was always so afraid of that, of something happening to her. But she never thought anything could happen, even when we used to̅ play down there."

"You played down there?"

"Well, of course, we weren't allowed to, but after your grandfather died, when Mother was trying to manage the factory herself, we pretty much had free rein. Lydia would follow me everywhere and I can't say I appreciated having my baby sister always tagging along, especially when I was hanging out with the boys. We'd hear the whistle and Lydia wouldn't get down from the rails. I'd finally have to yank her down, and she'd laugh and laugh when the train didn't come for another good five minutes. But she had more guts than all of us put together, even crossing that ridge."

"The Ridge? Mom crossed the Ridge?" Vickie had tried crossing it herself, but ended up by clinging to a Japanese pine at the top of the embankment until she mustered the courage to climb down.

"She was the only one able to make it. She knew to walk quickly so she wouldn't lose her balance. We knew too, but couldn't bring ourselves to do it." Uncle Warren laughed. "And how do you think I felt being outshone by my own baby sister?"

Vickie's mother had been so against her playing down there, it was hard to envision Lydia playing there herself, let alone crossing the Ridge.

"Do you think she thought that when she died? That nothing could happen?" Vickie asked.

Uncle Warren's gaze returned to the crack above the stove. "I don't know. Maybe she just never got over that, needing to take risks. Stupid risks."

Lydia had been so protective of Vickie, it was hard for Vickie to imagine her mother taking any real risks herself. She'd only ever been able to imagine her as the devoted daughter, and Vickie remembered what Uncle Warren had said when Ruth slapped him, about Lydia never before having disappointed her—or at least, not in any way that Ruth had ever known about, like the Ridge. Or Gail.

CHAPTER 27

VICKIE HADN'T been down to her old darkroom since she'd set up the one she used to have in the city. Everything was as it had been in high school except for the enlarger and processing tank she'd taken with her, things her father had helped finance as combination birthday and Christmas gifts. He'd built the darkroom partially enclosed beneath the stairs. Encrusted bottles of developer and fixing solution, as well as measuring and storage containers, still lined the shelves he'd bracketed to the back of the steps. The processing trays were in a row on the secondhand metal desk her father had picked up for her as a worktable. Going in there now, she was hoping that familiar refuge might help loosen the knot closing her throat since she'd found out about Meryl and Kyle.

That morning, her uncle and cousins had seemed more than ready to leave, especially Phillip who had the car completely packed before breakfast.

"Well, you take care of yourself in New York," Uncle Warren had said to Vickie, as if they'd never spoken the way they had in the middle of the night.

"Well, you, too," she said. "Take care."

"I'm sorry Meryl's not here to say good-bye, but she works today," Ruth said.

"Give her our love," Uncle Warren said, slipping his hand into his pocket, feeling for the watch.

Ruth slid her hands up and down her hips as if she longed for her own pockets, and Vickie thought how her grandmother and her uncle hadn't really talked since Ruth ran her Thunderbird into the spruce tree. How they probably had never really talked. Not even as much as she and Uncle Warren had, about the Ridge, about his fears of all that could ever have happened to his baby sister.

Vickie uncovered a pile of prints from her re-frigerator series and remembered the exhilaration of transforming the most ordinary of vegetables into something interesting, of creating a sense of dimension out of the perfect symmetry of a half grapefruit or a hard-boiled egg. Lighting had been everything, and she remembered going through roll upon roll of film to achieve the perfect intensity of shadow around an arrangement of pears.

It had been Kyle who showed her the trick of softening the shadows by propping white cards just outside the range of the lens. At the beach, he'd taught her how to precisely adjust the film-speed setting to prevent overexposure from the sand's reflection. He'd even built her a glass-bottomed box so that she could immerse her camera in the water to photograph the shifting shells and stones at low tide.

Missing him again, she was furious with herself, and she turned off the overhead bulb so that she was in pitch black; her favorite part of processing had been loading the film into the developing reel when there could not even be the amber glow of the safelight, and all feeling was routed toward her sense of touch.

Panicked now by the darkness as she had been by the underwater cave in Wheels Cove, she snapped back on the overhead bulb. She heard someone coming downstairs and was glad for an excuse to leave the darkroom.

It was Meryl. She must have just gotten off work.

"I was on my way over to Gail's to pick up the kids," she said, pausing halfway down the stairs.

Vickie didn't say anything.

"You've seen him, haven't you."

Now Vickie only wanted to retreat back into her darkroom.

"Do you think we can talk at all?" Meryl asked.

"I don't think I'm the one who has anything to say."

"Then can you listen? For a minute?" Meryl sat on the bottom step. "It doesn't make a lot of sense to me either. Not much more than it does to you."

"Don't tell me you couldn't help yourself."

Meryl stared at a spot on the cement floor, and Vickie remembered what Kyle had said about Meryl having been the one to ask herself over to his place.

"Then it *was* you?"

One of their father's shelves was lined with failed toys, and Meryl took down a discarded doll's head. She traced its mouth painted slightly askew.

"Why?" Vickie asked.

"I don't know."

"Don't stand there and tell me you don't know!"

"I *don't*. I told Glenn that, that I don't know. . . ."

"You must know *something*. There must be some reason you'd jeopardize your marriage, unless you've gone completely insane."

Meryl laughed. "Maybe that's it—I wanted to go insane."

"What the hell is this, Meryl? Who's doing all the hurting now? Look what you've done!"

"Yes, look what I've done. Look at what *I've* done."

"What, are you proud of this?"

"No. Just astonished. That this is me."

"It's not you. This isn't you."

"You know, it's funny. You and Glenn say all the same things—he doesn't think it's me either." Meryl sat on the step again, and balancing the doll's head on top of her knees, she said, "Maybe it is. Maybe this really is me."

"God, you're not even sorry, are you?"

"I guess I'm wishing I didn't have to be." Meryl let the head roll down her legs and bump across the floor. "I really didn't want to hurt anyone, Vickie."

"Yes, you did. You wanted to hurt me."

Meryl got up slowly, as if her joints ached, and went upstairs.

CHAPTER 28

MERYL DIDN'T KNOW WHY she'd thought Vickie might actually be able to understand. She supposed that she'd hoped Vickie would on some level be able to accept that Meryl herself didn't fully understand. Although when Meryl thought back on the affair now, she couldn't help looking back on it with a nostalgia for a feeling she hadn't known since sometime before she was married, when one night she couldn't sleep and lay beneath Ruth's cherry tree in full bloom. When she'd been able to open out into her own private vision of staring up through the brilliant collage of petals.

Daryll was playing in the sandbox, and Alex was swinging on the tire when Meryl arrived at Gail's to pick them up. The two remaining dogs lay together as if seeking solace in each other's bodily warmth.

"Hi, Mom," Alex called distractedly, humming a tune to herself.

"Hi, honey."

Meryl sat next to Gail on her patio. "Has she said anything to you?"

"About being in the barn? Only that really." Gail was sewing a pillow into its cover. "She certainly has a mind of her own."

"I know. And I wish I could see how it ticks."

"Well, all we mothers do. Our way of holding on, I guess. Or at least trying to."

Gail was actually ripping out the stitches, and Meryl asked, "You're starting over?"

"It's just all wrong."

She was wearing flip-flops, and Meryl was saddened by her having painted her hammertoes a frosty pink as if they could look anything but deformed. She'd almost forgotten about Clara, about how much she had meant to Gail.

"I'm thinking of leaving Glenn," Meryl said.

Gail, plucking out the snipped threads, didn't say anything for a moment. "And the kids?"

"I know. That's why I'm just thinking about it."

Gail only nodded, and Meryl said, "You're not at all surprised, are you?"

"I told you I thought something's been going on. Not just financial pressures. Anyway, I hope this isn't . . . well, that it's not finally over Clara. I mean, sooner or later something had to happen."

"Something?"

"Well, we have all been just kind of going along." Laughing a little, Gail said, "Although in our own strange ways maybe—who'd ever have thought I'd end up with a bevy of dogs?" Putting aside the pillow, she leaned back to contemplate them. "But they are rather beautiful, don't you think?"

Meryl didn't know whether they were beautiful, but in their stillness she felt that enormous gulf. This was how her mother had left them all, to sit so idly, and she wished now that her mother could actually have known about her affair with Kyle. She wished she could make her angry.

"What are you *doing?*" Lydia would have yelled incredulously, as she had the time Meryl smeared red nail polish across the divan. Meryl, only five, found the contrast of red against the divan's faded blue deeply gratifying, and she couldn't help but feel the least bit triumphant when her mother failed to rub out the stain.

The dogs shifted, shaking out their fur, then settled into new positions. Meryl envied their languidness, and she got up to pet them. It was the first time she'd touched the dogs, and she combed her fingers through their coats, feeling the fine differences in their textures.

Alex got off the swing to crouch beside her. "Watch how ticklish she is," she said, scratching Sage's belly so that her back legs quivered, and Meryl laughed.

"You try it," Alex said.

"How do you know she likes it?"

"Look at her tail thumping."

Scratching Sage's belly, Meryl asked, "What do you say we stop by and see Daddy?"

"At his house?"

Meryl laughed again as Sage's hind legs quivered, reminding her of her own children's ticklish spots.

There was no electricity last time Meryl had been by the house, and Glenn had to plug his tape deck into the truck's cigarette lighter. She could hear the blare of his jazz tapes coming from inside the house.

"Hey . . . ," he said confusedly, as they all filed in.

Meryl wandered around the big open living room trying not to feel like an intruder. Last time,

Glenn had been installing the floorboards, and now even the bricks of the fireplace were laid. Through the sliding glass doors, she could see that he'd begun arranging the scraps of sod he'd picked out from the dump.

"It looks great."

"Think so?" he asked.

Meryl hadn't considered before what it must be like for him working alone every day with only his music and his thoughts and the prospect of having to finish this tremendous undertaking singlehanded. "It really does, Glenn."

He couldn't help smiling. "Well, you might as well see the upstairs."

When they all came back down, Alex asked, "Can I play on the grass?"

"You can put some down if you like," Glenn said.

Alex went outside, and Daryll stomped around the living room, grinning at the sound of his own echo.

"So what made you come by?" Glenn asked.

"I told you I wanted to."

Glenn returned to what he'd been doing when they arrived, staining the trim around the windows.

Meryl sat on the floor against one of the sliding doors. "What are we going to do?"

He didn't say anything.

280

"We can't even talk about this, can we?"

"No. Not right now."

"Glenn . . . He really didn't mean something to me."

"I know."

Glenn came over and sat next to her. "If I *didn't* know, maybe I'd be better able to accept it. Like why you can't accept how I could shoot a dog in the first place."

Alex was patting down small squares of sod, and Meryl was reminded of how she used to make pancakes at the beach.

"Maybe we need time apart," Glenn said. "Maybe just a few days, a week. . . . I can stay here. I have everything I need—the plumbing even works."

Meryl pressed her hands against the floor to keep herself from spiraling downward. It seemed impossible now that she'd been the one thinking about leaving him.

Daryll seemed to have fallen into a trance, stomping in small overlapping circles.

"What will we tell Alex?" she asked.

"We'll tell her Daddy needs to finish up the house. Once and for all. There's just a lot we don't know about each other, Meryl. You'd think after all these years, but . . ." He went back to staining the windows.

Meryl grasped her knees as she cannonballed into the wake of her son's echo.

CHAPTER 29

RUTH HAD GONE back to bed again after Uncle Warren left, and late that afternoon, Vickie found her slumped against a mound of pillows, knitting either an exceptionally narrow scarf or an oblong pot holder.

"What are you doing?" Vickie asked.

"What does it look like I'm doing?"

"You don't knit, Gramma. You never did."

"How is it you know my own mind?"

Ruth pulled out more yarn from the tangled ball caught in her blankets, and it could have been those first few days after Lydia died. Vickie then had actually found some relief in the soft click of her grandmother's needles, and she'd once again been able to become engaged in the intricate details of those snuffboxes: the wooden ones painted with miniature scenes of waterfalls and parks; the silver one in the shape of a slipper; and her favorite, with a compass embedded in its lid. Ordinarily Ruth would have scolded her for opening the glass case, but either she hadn't noticed or simply hadn't cared.

Besides the snuffboxes, there were Ruth's great-great-grandmother's elaborate perfume dispensers, her embroidered evening purse displayed on the wall, and her long-stemmed hatpins arranged in a bud vase. All things that had given contour to a past Vickie had never known. But now in the wan light filtering through Ruth's thick lace curtains, the objects reeked of a past so alien they seemed to have belonged to no one who had ever actually existed. They belonged to those daguerreotypes in the buffet so faded now that Ruth's great-grandmother could only be seen when her ghostly silhouette was angled a certain way in the light. Nothing in that house actually belonged solely to Ruth, any more than it had to Vickie's mother. Feeling her own self fading, Vickie opened the curtains.

Ruth squinted at the sun.

"Mom wouldn't want this."

"What?"

"*This*. She would want you to get out of bed."

"Like she would want me to have that party?" Ruth said bitterly, fumbling at the neck of her nightgown for her bifocals. They'd fallen into her lap, and putting them on, she returned to her knitting.

She seemed so small and desiccated against the pillows, Vickie was suddenly infuriated. "You really would want her seeing you like this, looking so . . . old?"

Ruth opened her mouth as if to say something. Instead, she reached for the gnarled yarn, and gently tugging at a knot to untangle it, she seemed preoccupied in a way that was new. As if, finally, she was actually feeling her age.

"Can I bring you anything?" Vickie asked.

"What? Bring me what?"

"Anything. From downstairs."

Ruth pulled herself up so that she wasn't quite so slumped against the pillows. "I'm fine."

Gail's dogs were lying out back and they dispiritedly lifted their heads in greeting. Vickie found Gail sorting through a trunk of scrap material in her sewing room.

"I don't even know what I have here anymore," she said.

Vickie picked out a piece of material from the scraps Gail had flung onto the bed, a finely striped red-and-gold pattern she remembered from a dress with short ruffled sleeves. Gail had made all her own dresses before she began doing upholstery.

"I don't remember you ever not sewing," Vickie said.

"I know. But it surprises me these days how much I enjoy getting a seam wrong, just so I can rip it out."

It was hard to imagine Gail ripping out anything. Vickie remembered how much she enjoyed running her fingers back and forth along a perfectly straight seam.

Reminded of how her grandmother would probably end up by ripping out her scarf or pot holder, she said, "Gramma's knitting again."

"Oh, dear."

"Maybe it's all right. Maybe she really is . . . tired."

Gail sat on the bed to sort through the pile. "I wasn't quite myself, you know. At the party."

"You had a legitimate excuse."

"They're *dogs,* Vickie," Gail said. Vickie watched her as she seemed only to be rearranging the scraps.

"You know, Gramma just resents you having known Mom maybe better than she did."

"I didn't necessarily know her better. She wasn't easy to know."

"You knew how she really felt about my stealing money for that bus ticket."

Gail didn't say anything. Then glancing around the room, she said, "I should just sell this place. It's gotten too big even with the dogs."

"You've been here forever."

"Seems like that, doesn't it? Ray's room is even the way he left it, his old baseball banners on the walls. And I have some of Jeffrey's things. Small things, a couple of ties, cuff links." She laughed. "Mementos." She looked down at her flip-flops, wiggling her hammertoes, and—as if disgusted by them—crossed her feet beneath the bed.

"You did love him," Vickie said.

"Don't sound so surprised. But then again, no one's ever been able to understand that, except your mother."

"She was the one telling you for years to leave him."

"That doesn't mean she didn't understand. She knew things could only get worse, that's all. And of course, your grandmother was right. I should have left him years ago. But I was afraid of this. Of how this house can sometimes feel, like after he first left."

"When Mom was spending the night?"

Gail got up then and quickly stuffed all the scraps back into the trunk. "Well, she knew that, the feel of an empty house."

"She never lived alone. . . ."

"You don't have to live alone to feel alone."

Vickie hadn't thought of her mother as ever having been lonely. But thinking again about how she'd combed her fingers through Gail's hair, Vickie wondered if whatever may have happened between them didn't remain rooted in their initial tenderness. That tenderness of her mother wrapping Gail's bleeding hands in her own nightgown. And of Gail helping Lydia up through the woods after finding her sprawled in the leaves.

"You know, I have to be going out," Gail said.

"Out?"

"Shopping. The refrigerator's empty."

Vickie couldn't remember Gail ever before wanting her to leave. "I'm sorry."

"Sorry? No, I have nothing for tonight, that's all, not even for the dogs."

Vickie wasn't sorry. She only felt that she'd made some deep intrusion into something that never should have been her business in the first place. "I mean about Clara."

"Oh, she's at peace now, dear. I know that. She's at peace."

CHAPTER 30

GLENN HAD PACKED enough clothes for less than a week, but as soon as Meryl could no longer hear the knock of his truck, she felt the emptiness of their house as if there were still unexplored corners.

"He's almost finished anyway," Alex said, as if she too felt the emptiness. "He won't be gone long."

"No. Not long."

Alex twisted around the ladder on Daryll's plastic fire truck, the one he never played with. "But why does he have to sleep there? Why does he have to leave?"

"He hasn't left, honey," Meryl said, a different loneliness beginning to lodge itself within her. A loneliness she couldn't quite locate, not like the usual ache between her ribs.

"Are you sick?" Alex asked.

"Am I sick? No, I'm not sick."

"Why aren't you going to work then?"

"I thought I needed a day off," Meryl said, disarmed by how young Alex seemed, rolling the truck back and forth between her legs. "And I thought maybe we had some catching-up to do."

"Us?"

"So what would you like to do?"

"I don't know. . . ."

"We can do anything you want."

Putting aside the truck, Alex said defiantly, "I want to go to the Engels farm."

"The farm?"

"For arrowheads."

The old Engels farm was in the southeast part of town, what had been all farmland before the development of white stucco condominiums. The Engels farm had been sold off to a developer as well, but with the recession, construction was abruptly halted after only the circular road had been paved. In summer, children from the neighboring condominiums transformed the road into a roller rink.

Daryll embarked on his own small hole, scraping at the ground, and Meryl began digging as gingerly. She'd never been fond of any real outdoor work, although every year she'd been the one to help her mother prepare her garden and transplant trees.

With only a trowel, Alex stabbed vigorously at the earth. She had wanted to bring along a shovel, but Meryl had reasoned, "From the bulldozers, the land's already been churned up so any arrowheads could be right along the surface."

Since Alex's disappearance, Meryl had begun to watch her with a new carefulness, one as much curious as vigilant. She'd watch her at moments when Alex seemed consumed by her private thoughts, as she was when sorting through her makeup box or drawing invisible pictures on the car window.

"Why'd you do it, Alex?" Meryl now asked.

"Do what?"

"Spend the night out there."

Alex sprinkled a trowelful of dirt into a pile along side her hole.

"Was it to scare me?"

Alex looked at her. "Were you?"

"Yes. Very."

Alex gave her pile a satisfied pat.

"Anyway, you don't need to do that again, you know."

"I won't."

"I mean, you don't have to give me a scare."

Alex only nodded.

"And you know, I'm hoping you'll let me know if you're, well, at all unhappy."

"Unhappy?"

"Well, for instance, school." Meryl was surprised at how uncomfortable she felt trying to talk frankly with her own daughter.

"You don't have to ask so many questions," Alex said.

"Yes, I do—I'm your mother, I'll ask you as many questions as I want. I can't make you answer them. But I can ask."

"School's okay . . . ," she said vaguely.

"You don't have to go there."

Alex looked at her.

"It would maybe be hard to change in midstream, but—"

"I don't need to change schools, Mommy," Alex said, sounding tired of her mother's probing. She became engrossed in digging her hole, and for the first time, Meryl could envision her off on her bike scouring for things—how she could become engrossed then too. Perhaps she wasn't as lonesome as Meryl imagined.

Feeling oddly left out, Meryl concentrated on digging her own hole. She dug out a wide circle so that she could reach in with both hands. The earth's cool graininess soothed her palms, and she dug with a rush of energy she'd come to know only with Kyle, when she'd grind herself against him until she was thoroughly wet and open and not caring.

"If we dig deep enough, we'll reach the other side of the earth," Alex said, abandoning her own hole to help with her mother's.

"We'll have to be digging a long time," Meryl said. "But maybe . . ."

When Meryl used to help her mother transplant trees, Lydia would insist on digging the holes herself, and Meryl wondered whether she had felt like this. As if she could always dig deeper, as long as she could keep digging and digging without having to reach the other side of the earth.

"I think I see something," Alex said, peering down the hole. "I think I see people."

"People? From where?" Meryl asked.

"I'm not sure . . . maybe New York."

Meryl laughed. "New York?"

"They're waving at us."

"Well, then, wave back. It's the polite thing to do."

Alex waved down the hole and so did Daryll if only as an excuse to flap his hands.

Meryl waved too, and she felt her mother there. Not in the same way as when she'd glimpsed her partially hidden among the cattails along Kyle's driveway. In all her empathy, she was as tangible as if she were there kneeling beside them, waving down the hole.

CHAPTER 31

VICKIE FOUND MERYL sitting out back in a fold-up chair with her feet dangling in the baby pool.

"I stopped by work," Vickie said.

"I thought you would have left by now."

"You know I don't leave until after rush hour."

"Look!" Alex called, showing off her dirt-stained hands and knees. She was running back and forth through the sprinkler. "We were digging holes."

"Looking for arrowheads?" Vickie asked.

"Not really . . . ," Alex said, pressing her hands into the sprinkler's spray. "Just digging."

Vickie noticed Meryl's own hands and knees were equally dirty.

"Glenn's moved over to the house," Meryl said.

Vickie hadn't yet considered that, Glenn's leaving.

"Just for a few days. He thinks we need time apart."

"You're lucky it's just a few days," Vickie said.

Meryl tossed Daryll's rubber boat back into the pool. "What are you doing here, anyway?"

"I guess I didn't think you should get off so easy," Vickie said, although she wasn't sure exactly why she'd wanted to see her sister.

"It was all very stupid, Vickie."

"Not to you."

Meryl was wearing shorts and she smeared the dirt from her hands onto her thighs.

"So did you enjoy him?" Vickie asked.

"Alex, watch your brother for a minute, okay?" Meryl said, getting up. "Let's go inside."

"Don't tell me what to do."

Meryl looked at her curiously. "Would you *mind* coming inside?"

Meryl washed her hands and stirred a package of iced tea mix into a pitcher, noisily knocking the spoon against the glass.

"So did you?" Vickie asked.

"Did I what?"

"Enjoy him?"

Rarely had they ever talked about sex, and now it was wrestling with a foreign language.

"He didn't mean to me what he means to you, Vickie."

"Did you *enjoy* him?"

"Yes, Vickie. Yes, I enjoyed him."

Vickie began to feel as panicked as if she were immersed again in that black void of her old darkroom.

"It wasn't just the sex," Meryl said.

"So you *are* stuck on him?"

"You know I'm not, Vickie."

"Then is it Glenn? Are you that unhappy with Glenn?"

"No . . . I don't think it really has to do with Glenn. . . ."

"Then what *does* it have to do with? If it's not Glenn, and it's not to hurt me, then what the hell is it?"

"I don't know! I told you, I don't know. I was attracted to him. . . ."

"You said it wasn't just sex."

"It wasn't. It was that I was *surprised* that I was attracted. . . . I don't know, I don't know, I do not know! Damn it, Vickie, don't you think I wish I did know? Don't you think I'm afraid of losing Glenn?"

She sat at the table, breathing deeply as if to calm herself.

Vickie sat on the couch. How false the photographs beneath the glass seemed, like stage props.

"The funny thing is, I thought about leaving him," Meryl said. "Mostly I think now, what if he leaves me?"

She glanced out at Daryll in that distracted way their mother used to have of checking on them playing in the yard, and Vickie remembered how Meryl had sounded in the basement, as though she really did wish this could be her. Vickie had to look away from her sister, not willing to acknowledge some small corner where she was beginning to believe Meryl.

"I've made quite a mess, haven't I," Meryl said.

"You like the mess."

Meryl looked at her.

"Well, you've always been so damn neat, haven't you?"

"Yes, Miss Neat," Meryl said, gesturing around at the clutter. "And what would Mom think? She'd be gravely disappointed, wouldn't she?"

"You don't have to sound so pleased."

"I'm not pleased. . . . I just mean if anything would have sent her over the edge, this would have."

"You think she'd actually take her own life because of you and Kyle?"

"I meant figuratively, Vickie, that she would be shocked."

Among the photos, there was one of Meryl and their mother sitting together with their feet dangling in the baby's pool. Lydia is gazing at something outside the frame. Her hands are unusually still in her lap, and Vickie longed for her to come in now, waving them in one of her wide, sweeping gestures. "It doesn't much matter anyway, does it, what she would think?"

"Then why should it matter about the train?" Meryl asked.

"Maybe it shouldn't."

"No? And since when?"

"Well, what *can* it change?"

Meryl nodded vaguely, and Vickie didn't remember her sister ever looking so uncertain. Not since they would sit huddled together on the landing listening to their parents argue downstairs. But the fact remained: they could never know what actually had been going through their mother's mind at that moment when the train was coming. Just as Vickie could never know exactly why she had been lonely, nor for certain what had been the true nature of her relationship with Gail.

What Vickie did know was that her mother's friendship with Gail had run deeper than she'd ever thought possible—that her mother had been capable of a depth Vickie had underestimated. A depth even

Meryl seemed not to have been able to realize, despite all the time they had spent together doing jigsaw puzzles on Sunday afternoons, sitting on the counter licking batter from a bowl, or dangling their feet in that pool.

How lonely Meryl herself seemed now, licking one finger to draw streaks through the dirt on her thighs. As lonely as when she cupped her face against the window, and Vickie found herself missing her. Missing her in a way she wasn't ready to accept. "I need to get packed."

"Oh . . . ," Meryl said, glancing at her watch, sounding a little disappointed. "I think Alex really wants to visit you in New York," she said. "Maybe sometime we can work something out."

"Maybe."

As she was going out the door, Meryl said, "Kyle really loves you, Vickie. You have to know that."

CHAPTER 32

WHEN VICKIE GOT HOME from her sister's, Ruth not only was up and dressed but serving tea to Kyle and from her best cups, the ones decorated with yellow butterflies.

"Well, he dropped by and I thought you'd be back soon," Ruth explained.

Kyle seemed ungainly pinching the cup's tiny handle.

"He's been telling me about his garden. Did you know bugs can be fooled?"

"Yes, Gramma."

"Anyway, he wanted to see you before you left—"

"He can speak for himself, Gramma."

Kyle neatly folded his linen napkin beside his saucer. "Would you mind going for a short drive, to the beach?"

"It's lovely this time of day," Ruth said.

"I talked to Meryl," Vickie said, once they were walking along the beach. "Glenn's left."

"Oh, shit."

"What did you expect?"

"Well, maybe they just need time. I mean, they've been together for years. . . ."

"Don't try injecting logic into all of this, Kyle."

He stopped in front of her. "Then quit acting like I cheated on you, Vickie. If we were together, you think I'd let this happen? And if it wasn't Meryl, it would have been somebody else."

"It *was* Meryl."

"I know, and I'm sorry, and I can't tell you that enough," he said, sitting in the sand. "Damn it, Vickie, you keep ramming us up against a wall. You can punish me all you like, but it won't get you and me anywhere. Except right where we are now. Up against a goddamn wall."

Vickie waded into the tide. She watched the water move in and out around her feet until her ankles disappeared into the sand. Her clothes grew damp in the ocean's spray and she began to shiver, but she felt rooted there. As rooted as if she had always been standing there. Kyle was drawing circles in the sand, and looking back at him, her one constant, she saw how she'd never really left that town.

She went and sat beside him.

"Maybe we should just call things off," Vickie said.

"We did. Two years ago."

"No, really. I mean, not be in touch at all."

"God, Vickie."

"We can't be friends, Kyle. It hasn't worked."

"It has worked, until now, if we can maybe get past this. . . ."

"It isn't only this."

"Well, we don't have to end up in the back of the van, if that's what you mean."

"The thing is, I always want that, to end up in the back of the van."

"Even now?"

She drew her own circles in the sand. "I don't know." She only knew that she still loved him. "But you were right. I've just been putting on a show."

"I don't know that I was right."

"You were."

He could only nod, his eyes brimming, and she drew more circles in the sand, one overlapping the other, knowing they both wanted to be holding each other now. But if she were to make a single move toward him, she wouldn't be able to go through with this, to finally let him go. She would remain as rooted there as she was when she would imagine seeing her mother in New York at Woolworth's, the bank, or the Laundromat, in the most ordinary of places.

"I found some of my old prints," she said, for something to say. "They're not half bad."

"So I've told you."

"I know. I just needed to hear it from myself." Wiping out the circles, she said, "Maybe we should get going."

"God, Vickie."

"I know. Let's just get going, okay?"

They bent to pick up dried seaweed, stones, broken shells, anything to fill their hands.

CHAPTER 33

WHEN VICKIE GOT HOME, Ruth was sitting outside in her Thunderbird. Before Uncle Warren left, he and Phillip and Blake had managed to push the car back up to its original nesting place in front of the house.

Not wanting to be alone, Vickie got into the passenger seat, asking, "So what's new with the Arnolds?"

Ruth looked as startled as if Vickie had walked in on her getting dressed. "Mrs. Arnold came out wearing a terry-cloth robe," Ruth said, rearranging herself. "Maybe they're not Mafia after all."

"Because she was wearing terry cloth?"

"*I* wear terry cloth."

The size of the clock, radio buttons, and speed-ometer seemed as exaggerated as if the car were only pretend.

"I can't decide whether it's worth having the headlight repaired," Ruth said.

"If you're going to fix anything, I'd go for the brakes."

Ruth frowned. "Well, I don't really know why I bought it, anyway."

"You always wanted a T-bird."

"Your uncle's right, the bottom's rusted through."

"He's not right about everything."

Ruth looked at her. Then she said, "You know, you had this terrible game you used to play when you were small—you'd crawl into some small place like between the highboy and the chest, and we'd call and call for you. Your mother knew you'd come out eventually and said we should ignore you until you grew bored. But I was always the one to find you. I was the one to drag you out of your little hiding places."

Vickie was taken aback by her grandmother sud-denly telling her this. She played with the dial on the radio that didn't work.

"Anyway, you know I don't mean half the things I say, don't you?"

"Yes, you do."

Ruth ran her hands back and forth along the dashboard. Then slapping the dashboard, she said, "Silly old car." She got out, slamming the door. She went around to the side of the house.

Vickie sat there a moment longer. She could still see Kyle drawing circles in the sand, and she felt a loneliness she couldn't remember. Not even when she used to cry in the recesses around the cellar windows. Not even when she'd be longing so for her mother.

Ruth came back around lugging Blake's pail. Encased in the car's silence, Vickie watched her pluck out a drowned rat by its tail and, with the fluidity of moving through water, fling the rat into the woods alongside the house. Ordinarily whenever there was a dead mouse or bird, she would have called for Blake.

Vickie interlocked her fingers, trying to find some comfort in the feel of her own clasp.

TYLER

Tyler
After Lydia.

April 1995